# Grace and other stories

# Grace and other stories

by

Bongani Sibanda

Published by

Weaver Press, Box A1922, Avondale, Harare,
Zimbabwe. 2016
<www.weaverpresszimbabwe.com>

© Bongani Sibanda, 2016


Cover Design: Farai Wallace, Harare
Typeset by Weaver Press
Printed by RockingRat, Harare

ISBN: 978-1-77922-294-7 (p/b)
ISBN: 978-1-77922-295-4 (ePub)

**Bongani Sibanda** was born in Mfila Village and attended Zwehamba and Nyashongwe Primary Schools, then Tshelanyemba and Shashane High Schools. He currently lives in Johannesburg. His stories have appeared in several online literary magazines, and have been included in two of Weaver Press' anthologies, *Writing Lives* (2014) and *Writing Mystery and Mayhem* (2015). Sibanda was longlisted for the 2015 ABR Elizabeth Jolley Short Story Prize for 'Musoke', a fictionalised account of Uganda's Dominic Ongwen. He is currently writing a novel.

# Contents

# Grace

When the old minibus dropped him at Koba bus stop, Mlungisi felt as if he'd landed in heaven. Ten years without visiting home had made him not just homesick, but crazy.

The spring sun was low in the cloudless sky. A large herd of goats with loud irritating bells guided by two barefooted boys passed him as he bent down, dusting his trousers. Then he folded back the turn-ups of his pants and the cuffs of his blue shirt and pulled out the handle of his suitcase while waiting briefly for the dust caused by the goats to settle. Then, dragging his case, he walked westwards down the little brown footpath which he could clearly remember despite the many years he'd been away

His journey from South Africa had been well, uneventful, except for the hundred rand that corrupt immigration officers had made him pay at the border claiming his asylum had expired. And the brief delay in Harare, although he had, finally, acquired his passport. One thing Mlungisi loved about himself was his ability to get things done under any circumstances.

He looked about, enjoying the familiar strange sights; long stretches of land carpeted with overgrazed brown grass, a donkey and its foal grazing quietly to his left under a lone amarula tree. It felt blissful to be home at last where he could relax easily. South Africa had never felt like home what with all the studying he'd had to do. Nonetheless, that country had done well to show him that he needed a metamorphosis to become a part of the world in which he aspired to live in: a world of money, liberty and multiple options.

Before him, to his left, was the Koba homestead. It was still the same, with its three rondavels painted yellow, and a single-roomed, metal-sheeted brick house. Mlungisi could swear that the ramshackle scotch-cart under the lemon tree next to the front rondavel was in exactly that position when he'd left home a decade previously. He'd once bumped into Daisy, Koba's son, in the streets of Jo'burg, not long after he'd arrived, and they'd sat down and reminisced about their primary school days.

Mlungisi was a tall young man with a long freckled face, narrow shoulders, and his father's very pointed chin. His features blended those of his mother, an Ndebele, with those of his Shona father, whom he hated because, at fifty-one, he'd married his mother, who was sixteen at the time; then divorced her and thrown her out into the street: abuse that Mlungisi found unforgivable. However, his mother was now settled well in Johannesburg, which was how Mlungisi had managed to pursue his studies without the pressure of working like other Zimbabwean youngsters who migrated south. Now he was home for the first time in ten years, to collect his passport and visit his grandparents. But more than that, he was hoping he would meet a beautiful girl with manners, to court and then marry. He felt that the time was ripe, but he was not keen on dating materialistic South African women. His sister, Manto, had tagged along when she heard that he was going home. She'd preceded him into the village while he waited for his passport in Harare. She had promised that she would look around for a wife for him. That was the nature of their relationship – brother and sister looking out for one another.

There was a new home on the other side of the street near Na-Doris', his grandparents' neighbours. It was already dark when Mlungisi reached there, but this new homestead, with a white van parked in the courtyard, had a white globe hanging in front of a big, asbestos-roofed house, and it shone over a wide area. Sungura music poured out of the building.

When he finally arrived at his grandparents' homestead he was greeted by the noise of children playing, and fires flickering inside his grandparents' yard, and he knew at once that the Dawus and the Tshumas were there. A church service was in process.

His heart skipped nervously as he stood at the gate, thinking again about what Marshal, an old school mate had told him in the minibus. He and Marshal had never really been friends but in a shared moment on the journey from Harare, Marshal had said his dream was to go to South Africa to fulfil his ambition. This, it seemed to Mlungisi, had amounted to male prostitution, but he'd said nothing.

Mlungisi had always disliked people like Marshal who was rich and spoiled. As a young boy, he had not understood where his hostility to Marshal had come from, but now he realised it was a dislike for people with natural advantages, handsome and born into well-to-do families; people who made the world seem more unfair to others. To people like him.

'I told Lethiwe that the Mlungisi I know would be here before sunset,' Grandmother NaTimoty said as she led the young man from the gate, dragging his suitcase on its wheels down the dusty courtyard. 'You must be exhausted, Lethiwe's son?'

'Oh hardly, Grandma,' Mlungisi said. 'I feel like I've been relaxing all day.'

Accompanying his grandmother and smiling broadly, was Manto, who was holding hands with her friends Tamara, Nshiye and Elizabeth, all of whom Mlungisi had known since they were young girls, playing with rag dolls, and painting their lips sooty with coals. Grandmother NaTimoty was leading the way to her house, turning every second as if to check that her grandson had not disappeared.

'Your mother calls almost every day,' she said. And before Mlungisi could reply, continued, 'My God, I can't believe how big you are. What does your mother feed you on? Your grandfather would be surprised. He is out looking for goats with King. I don't suppose you know King, a youngster who came looking for work years ago. And you know your grandfather. Couldn't say no. He's been here now for almost six years.'

The homestead was new, Mlungisi noticed, and larger than the previous one, and constituted an assortment of mud huts and brick houses, about ten or eleven in all, a few plastered, none painted. They were spread haphazardly across the large courtyard like bones on a shaman's sack. As they walked across the spacious open area, Mlungisi also noticed more people than he remembered. To his right, in front of an unpainted four-cornered house, roofed with corrugated iron sheets, a group of children were noisily singing and dancing in the dark. To the right, in front of the hut closest to the field, which shared fencing with the homestead, a large fire blazed, and old men were seated on small stools, talking as loudly as the old women in a rondavel on the other side, where fire could be seen through the narrow door.

'Grandpa thought you were no longer coming, Mlu,' Manto said. 'He thought that you'd got your passport and headed back to SA.' She giggled.

'How like him,' Mlungisi scoffed absent-mindedly.

Mlungisi loved his little sister, his only sister by his mother, who'd only had three children; she'd been the last born, the baby. Now nineteen, she was a tall, slim girl with an attractive figure, and a good heart; she epitomised the kind of woman Mlungisi wished to marry. His half-brother, a womaniser and a drunk, he did not care for at all.

The four of them stood near the wooden door of Grandmother NaTimoty's brick house, while she put Mlungisi's case inside. She had ordered them to wait outside because, as she put it, something serious was going on inside. For a moment, Mlungisi felt a wave of discontent and disorientation wash over him. He was also feeling nervous. Manto was telling him how lucky they were that a man called Mangarayi, a malayisha, was going to Bulawayo on Sunday morning; she'd asked for a ride and he'd agreed to take them, so they were not going to have to wake up very early to catch the bus. But Mlungisi was not listening. He was thinking about what Marshal had said, and about how, in an area like this, even with the best will in the world, you could never study, what with so much darkness and noise.

'Manto tells me Given hasn't changed,' Grandmother NaTimoty

said, shutting the door behind her, and heading towards the rondavel at the back.

'He's still the same, Grandma,' Mlungisi said, 'There's nothing
you can tell him.'

Grandmother NaTimoty shook her head, 'I feel so sad for Lethiwe.'

They paused in the courtyard, in front of the rondavel that was
bustling with old women. Mlungisi looked east, and saw yet again,
as he'd often done when he was a young boy, the three reddish dots,
that were the Ndabankulu Clinic tower lights. The clinic was close
to the high school that Mlungisi had attended. He'd found distant
relatives in the area and lived with them. Most children in the
neighbourhood went to high school by bicycle, or not at all.

Looking to the north, south and west, Mlungisi was surprised by
the darkness. It felt strange that he'd grown up in a place like this.
He thought he'd never get used to so much darkness, even if he were
to stay at home for a year. But Manto, all smiles, seemed to have
instantly adapted.

'Guess what's happening in Grandma's house,' she startled him
out of his reverie. Skipping about, she pulled at his arm, and made
as if she was going to jump on his shoulders, childish habits that
she'd not lost in her excitement.

'I don't know, what's happening?'

'Big mouth,' Grandmother NaTimoty said.

'It's no secret, Grandma,' Manto objected, and continued to tell
Mlungisi that in their grandmother's house was Musa, their aunt,
and two of Dawu's daughters, Maria and Akwira, who were accused
of cooking and eating mopane worms. With them was Pastor Joshua of Gohole, soliciting confessions and instructing them in verses
against eating such worms.

It was always a great affair, the weekend Vangwato sect gather-
ings. Mlungisi was glad to see a meeting so packed, though he no
longer considered himself a member. The Dawus, Tshumas and
Ngulubes, all of whom lived on the other side of Ngwesi River, had
all come out in force, and his relatives, all Mlungisi's uncles, with
their own homes, also attended. Sometimes, as this evening, people
from other sect branches arrived as well, especially the prophets

and young men from Bidi village, who were known for their loud eloquent singing voices.

At 3 p.m. on Fridays, members of the sect stopped working wherever they were, respecting the hour on which Jesus was crucified, though it was emphasised that Jesus was not the Messiah here, but Muzi, the sect founder and alleged reincarnation of John the Baptist, who'd been specially dispatched from Heaven to free Africa from colonialism.

At 6 p.m., everyone was expected to have arrived at SaTimoty's. This was where the service was held because he was the eldest and most senior priest. Then the people would cluster themselves, and sit according to peer groups. Young women, omakoti, filled the kitchen, which was a small unroofed mud shack, and cooked, after which they carried food to their families at different sites. By nine, everyone was expected to be in the big rondavel, which was where the service, which sometimes went on through the night, was held.

Mlungisi went to greet everyone, his aunts, uncles, his grandfather, SaTimoty, and other pastors. There was a lot of fussing, some asking him if he'd married and others, to his consternation, asking him when he would go to visit his father in Kezi. He preferred those who asked him about his studies, praised him for his hard work, and laughingly offered him their daughters, though he knew such suggestions weren't entirely a joke. He would be accepted with open arms if he offered himself as a son-in-law because his future was promising.

After supper, he and his grandmother went to sit in her house. Pastor Joshua's little sermon was over.

'Are you sure you won't need anything stronger, Lethiwe's son?' Grandmother NaTimoty asked. Mlungisi had declined the sadza.

'No, I'm fine, Gogo. Really, I am. I had a take-away on the bus. And where the hell is Manto? Where the hell is she?'

'Gone to sleep,' said Grandmother NaTimoty. 'They do that. She and her friends. They wake up later when the service has started; so that they don't get to drowse during the service'

Grandmother NaTimoty lit a paraffin lamp and placed it on a wooden bench. They sat on her bed. On the other side was grandfather SaTimoty's single bed. A certain disorder filled the rest of the house: old bags with old clothes nobody wore lay scattered around. Why did his grandmother keep all those old garments, Mlungisi wondered, something he'd never thought about before he went to South Africa.

'And tell me, Mlungisi,' Grandmother NaTimoty said softly, her head bent close to Mlungisi as if she wanted to bite his nose off. 'What's this I hear about you taking Tshuma's son with you? Explain yourself, young man.'

'You've got the facts correctly, Gogo. Sunday I'm leaving with Abraham, that is if Tshuma will allow me.'

'And why are you doing that, pray tell me?'

'I'm helping them out, Gogo, why else?'

'And why are you helping them out, Lethiwe's son? Have you thought this through?'

'Why, perfectly,' Grandmother NaTimoty shook her head and clapped hands together, muttering.

'What now, Gogo? Do you think it's wrong of me?'

'Have you thought about how this will make your aunts feel? They too want to go to South Africa. You're aware of that, yes?'

'Well, I don't care what they think, Gogo. It's about helping out the Tshumas. Where is Abraham, by the way? I haven't seen him since I arrived.'

'Abraham works at Lubangwe. He will be here tomorrow. Tshuma is on his way now. He remains behind, penning the goats since all his children are away.'

Grandmother NaTimoty was a short woman, with very few teeth. She wore a white headscarf, beneath which a little grey hair peeped. Her face was more wrinkled than it had been three years ago when she visited Mlungisi and his mother in Johannesburg.

The young man had known his grandmother better than he'd known his mother, after the latter had literally stolen her children from their father and taken them to live with their grandparents when they were seven, four and two. She had never joined them, being always away at the mines peddling and hawking fruits to educate them. Later, she'd left for South Africa, still leaving her children in their grandparents' care. Like all their other grandchildren, they'd been raised by the Bible, inured to the stoic life of farming and herding during the winter cold, and made to understand, first hand, the principle that in life, you eat what you work for. Sometimes Mlungisi's grandfather, whom the youth still secretly resented, was bold enough to question Mlungisi about whether he would eat books when he found his grandson hiding between millet stocks reading instead of watching to ensure that the birds weren't eating the crops. Now the fruits of that rebellion were beginning to manifest themselves; he was close to acquiring a political science degree.

That night, he talked about many things with his grandmother: planting, the rains, aid from World Vision, which had since disappeared, the woes of the people who had no relatives in South Africa, and how much better it was now that Mlungisi's mother and uncles were contributing some money every month for groceries. And then they talked about the service, his grandmother telling him about the people who'd come, the Bidi boys, the Gohole and Ntobe prophets – though Mlungisi had seen them all – and how great the service would be. Then Grandmother NaTimoty expressed sadness over the bad blood between Mlungisi's mother and Elvis, one of Mlungisi's uncles, a feud which had gone on far too long.

'And why do you have to go so soon, Lethiwe's son, tell me?' Grandmother NaTimoty complained. Really, Sunday is tomorrow. You haven't seen us. Have you seen us? No.'

'Because, Gogo, I've to go back to school, that's why.'

They went outside when Pastor Tshuma started calling people to assemble for the service. They were now talking about Mlungisi's younger brother, Given, and how sad it was that he'd left school and chosen to become a drunkard.

'Your mother is proud to have you,' Grandmother NaTimoty said.

'Everything I've achieved is due to her, Gogo.'

'I just don't understand why you don't sit down with your brother and educate him about the importance of life. I mean, the necessity of taking responsibility. He'll regret himself, Mlungisi, don't you see that? He will envy you.'

They saw Tshuma pass close by, shouting, and hurried to the rondavel where people were beginning to assemble for the service because they knew he didn't like it when people ignored his call.

'I wonder when he arrived,' Grandmother NaTimoty asked raising her eyebrows.

Pastor Tshuma was a tall man with long veiny arms, and a very tanned face as he lived by mending fences from which he was paid with food and clothes. Mlungisi thought that taking Abraham, his son, to help him find a job in South Africa, would probably improve their lives.

Slowly people began to gather in the big rondavel, indifferent to Pastor's Tshuma's urgent entreaties. There were some whom Mlungisi had not greeted, and he did so now. Among them was SaEdwardi from Matemani. He was the wealthiest and most handsome man in the village, and had by far the ugliest, meanest wife. Turning the focus on Mlungisi, he announced that he'd heard how well the young man was doing in South Africa, and how he should be an inspiration to all the young people in the village.

'You take after your mother,' he continued, 'That girl Lethiwe is very wise. You would not believe how well she has done for herself in Jo'burg.'

'I was there two years ago, SaEdwardi,' Grandmother NaTimoty broke in. 'I couldn't believe the house she had bought, how she's got herself a fine job, and so much property. Lethiwe is a remarkable child.'

SaEdwardi, though not SaTimoty's son, was always regarded as if he were. They had raised him, after he came looking for work. Though he later bonded with his father and built a home near him at Matemani, he had not forgotten the people who had brought him up and had remained a member of the Vangwato sect.

Meanwhile Dawu asked Mlungisi when he was going to get married – didn't he realise that girls were waiting for him. Flushed, Mlungisi stood dumb, until Pastor Tshuma rescued him as he complained that everyone was ignoring his call to the service.

Mlungisi was still discomposed by the girls Manto had shown him. Manto, enthusiastic, had first shown him Tamara, and Mlungisi had felt short-changed. Tamara, with her drooping lower jaw and dirty bare feet, was far from what Mlungisi had imagined would be a perfect fit for him.

Then Manto had shown him other available girls -- Elizabeth and Nshiye. They too were dirty and below his standards. And he had realised that he would have to return to South Africa without finding the gorgeous village girl of his dreams.

'There should be punishment for people who do this,' Pastor Tshuma shouted. 'These girls, these young women, they act like my call is not for them… and I will not have it.'

Some people laughed. Tshuma's petulance was a standing joke. Mlungisi remembered how he often worked himself into a passion over nothing.

'We should call Boxer,' Dawu suggested with a sly grin.

Everyone began giggling. Boxer was a fat policeman from a nearby police camp known for whipping young delinquents, especially school children who disrespected their teachers or flunked. He had fallen out of grace, however, when news emerged that he'd been beaten by his shopkeeper girlfriend, for cheating on her. So everything said of him was marked by this little detail.

The congregants began to take positions, elderly woman at the back near the door, and elderly men to the east, facing the women. The middle was occupied by young people – all facing the east.

Dawu started the song 'Giroriya', which she unaccountably sang as a dirge. Standing at the front, Pastor Tshuma kept gesturing for people to start a new song.

And then, at last, sitting down, he asked for the opening hymns. There were three – 'Osana', 'Alleluyah' and 'Giroriya' – and they were sung in that order, with everyone seated.

'Peace be with everyone,' Pastor Tshuma began, when the opening songs had ended. Then he spoke lengthily about the necessity of attending the service every Saturday, warning the congregants that if you miss one weekend, you'll then miss the next and before you know it, you'll find yourself not attending church at all.

'Because,' he said, raising his voice a little. 'Distractions will always be there, *bazalwane*. It is Satan's job to keep creating them and hurling them your way. Your responsibility is to stand up to them.'

Mlungisi felt as if the warning was directed at him and his mother. They never went to church. Not even when a branch of the Vangwato sect was established in Alexandra, not far from where they lived.

'The angels in heaven are watching as you bath on Saturday,' Pastor Tshuma shouted. 'As you weed on Saturday, as you go about collecting debts and visiting heathens on Saturday; they are watching and they complain to Jehovah because during their times, during the times of Enoch, Moses and Abraham, during the times of Daniel, Mishack and Abednigo, men were killed for such things. Men were killed for not observing the Sabbath. You've it easy now, Africans. You've it easy indeed. So I urge you my brethren. I urge you to observe the Sabbath day. It's not mine, it's not Pastor Tshuma's, it's not Pastor SaTimoty's. Don't go weeding saying as long as Pastor Tshuma won't see me, it's all right. Jehovah sees you and he is the one who will be judging you, not Pastor Tshuma or SaTimoty. We're just his messengers.'

He had planned to continue but someone started singing. It a was young woman. She sang with a nice voice, slowly and patiently. Curious to know who was singing, Mlungisi glanced back. It was Tamara, SaEdwardi's daughter, he'd heard about how well she was doing at school. Unlike her father, she was dark-skinned. He would like a girl who was bright at school, but her physical appearance turned him off.

When she stopped someone else began another song, which was sung in a lively manner, but Mlungisi was failing to connect with the service. He found himself thinking about his books, his life, even the world news. Recently, he'd read about the earthquake in Nepal, about a village that had been obliterated and it had upset him. He imagined it being his village and he being consumed by the quake and felt that it would have been very unfair. He had a vivid imagination – structures being destroyed and crashing down on people, the screams, the wounded, dead, it all seemed very real to him.

Meanwhile the song was heating up. The young men from Bidi

had risen to their feet and had inspired many others to do the same. Known for their loud voices, they sang with their hands resting on their cheeks, pacing about, eyes closed and mouths wide open. Some started speaking in tongues as Jesus' disciples had done at Pentecost. Mlungisi had since found out that it was not only the Vangwato sect that encouraged this, but many other churches did as well. The only difference was that at Vangwato only a select few were considered to have second sight.

There was a little whispering at the front when the enthusiastic singing came to an end. Then Pastor Tshuma announced that Pastor SaTimoty had something to say. On his feet, SaTimoty pulled his white wrap-around tighter around his body, rubbed his hands together and uttered: 'May happiness be with you, servants of Jehovah.'

'Amen,' the congregants shouted cacophonously.

SaTimoty had a screechy voice like someone with laryngitis and in that voice he told them that he had gone 'there' – meaning Ntumbane, Bulawayo, the church's headquarters, where the lord, honourable Bishop Mkandla, was very happy to receive the financial contributions from Malaba, though, he had pointed out, they were less than other branches had given. SaTimoty urged the congregants to all try and contribute more to keep up with other churches.

He then talked about the issue of the transport money, how he had had to draw from his own pocket when he was submitting the contributions for the whole church. Pastor Tshuma interrupted SaTimoty to say that he had previously spoken about this issue:

'It isn't fair' he said, 'that Baba SaTimoty should spend his own money when he's doing things for the whole church. You mustn't forget,' he told the congregants, 'that your tithes have to be transported and transport is money.'

An elderly woman at the back tried to begin a melancholy song, but Pastor SaTimoty was undeterred. He announced the Bishop's plans to buy a new farm called Mashukela, formerly owned by a white man, who had left for Europe. This was followed by wild applause and ululations. In consequence, a middle-aged man started a song, 'This church is heading far, far beyond the mountains.'

A few people rose and danced. It was a cheerful song. Mlungisi meant to rise, but he could not bring himself to do so until the song ended. SaTimoty then announced the Bishop's plans to buy an aeroplane.

There was a legend about three properties of the Vangwato sect which had been stolen by a white colonialist from Muzi, the Vangwato sect founder. And so news of the aeroplane meant the reclamation of those properties, which would precede the Vangwato sect's dominance of all other world churches, including the Catholic Church, and this was about to happen. The properties were a sleeveless jacket, a club that could sing on its own, and the Bible that gave an African account of God's interaction with black people.

Lastly, before he sat down, Pastor SaTimoty reiterated the Bishop's call that members of the Vangwato sect should not be swayed by suffering and stand united with the revolutionary party.

'It is the white man who makes us suffer, so we will turn against our liberators, and thus give him power to oppress us again,' he said. 'But that will end. Jehovah will end it. The same way he ended colonialism. Nothing under the sun is bigger than He.'

Someone started the song, 'Ayikho enye inkosi enganqob' uBaba', no other king could conquer Jehovah.

The fire was burning brightly in the hearth but for someone unused to it, Mlungisi found the smoke unbearable. He rose and went outside into the fresh air. Slowly, he walked towards the gate, enjoying the air but feeling nervous. He had not entirely outgrown his fear of ghosts, witches and demons, associated with darkness in the village. Feeling a little thirsty, he went in search of water, and found a twenty-litre chigubu in the shack where food was prepared. He wondered why, if witches were so malicious, they did not sneak into places such as the shack and simply poison the water. Why did their methods always seem so strenuous and elaborate. Was it easier and safer to travel on a broom?

Leaving the hut, he sauntered in front of the boys' house, where children had been playing earlier. The moon, shining brightly, was two hours into the dark sky.

He was still discomposed by the girls who were far from what he had expected. At sixteen, Tamara looked like NaEdwardi, her mother. For him, beauty was as important as good manners in a woman. And all the girls his sister had shown him were ugly. Perhaps he would see others the next day.

He saw a woman come out of the kitchen, and walk straight towards him. It was his sister.

'What are you doing here?' She sat down next to him.

'Just getting some fresh air.'

'Gogo still hopes we'll stay a little longer. But Mlu, why don't we…'

'No, God, I told you we can't,' Mlungisi snapped. 'Geez, I've to get back to school.'

'Pity! I would have found you a superb girl if we stayed another week.'

He looked at her without blinking. She was smiling and he smiled too. He was happy as long as she was happy. Their unconditional love cleaned his spirit.

'Tamara blushes when I mention you.'

Mlungisi did not reply.

'She can't be that bad. Come on, Mlu!'

Again he did not reply. Then they began to talk about the service, what they'd seen various prophets do, exclaiming and marvelling over their words and deeds. But Mlungisi knew he was only keeping the conversation going. He was as disenchanted with the service as a cat at a wedding.

Then his sister reminded him that they had to get back. 'People will talk,' she told him, and he knew it well.

When they returned, they found Prophet Khumalo of Ntobe prophesying people one by one. A woman called MaDube from Lubangwe was standing attentively before him, her hands folded across her chest.

'Pray hard,' the prophet told her as they came in and sat down. 'Praying hard is the only thing that will lift you to victory. It is no weak spirit I'm talking about. You should pray very hard.'

Mlungisi was still a young boy when a prophet from Binga told Dawu that she was a witch, and responsible for her husband's illness. Dawu's husband, Pastor Nyoni, was still alive then. Pandemonium had ensued, Dawu accusing Pastor SaTimoty of having called 'those people' to cause trouble in her marriage. Mlungisi hoped nothing like that would happen tonight.

Many people were prophesied. Some were told of how their evil neighbours were trying to block their successes, and how their lack of faith was giving Satan access in their lives. Others were told about dirty spirits trying to interfere and influence their lives, and how they needed to attend church frequently, if they were to overcome such deeds.

Mlungisi thought that Prophet Khumalo actually changed when he was in a trance. Several prophets stood up, and one of them, a big-headed young man from Bidi, said there was a huge, evil-smelling dragon living in SaTimoty's goats' kraal. He said the dragon flew across the homesteads of the worshippers at night, breathing bad air, which caused sickness among babies and conflict among the members of the church. Its foul breath spread across villages increasing in volume and rapacity, the further it spread, blocking out rain, causing disease, and maintaining a state of disharmony among the country's political leaders.

'It is up to you, *bazalwane*, to save our country. That is what you chose when you chose to be members of this church – that you'll spend sleepless nights righting wrongs. For this is a church mandated from the beginning of time with the task of righting all the earthly wrongs for the good of mankind.'

Mlungisi hoped that no prophesy be directed at him; he hated being the centre of attention.

Led by Khumalo, those gifted with the second sight crawled on their knees and converged at the front, where young men and women had to move a little to give room. Crowded around, they spoke in incoherent tongues, supposedly Hebrew, Aramaic and all the Middle Eastern ancient languages, because it was presumed that it were the angels, biblical persons, speaking through them. Dawu's angel was Prophet Ezekiel, son of Buzi; Khumalo's was Caleb, son of Jephunneh. There was a young man from Bidi screaming the most and his angel was believed to be Daniel. They talked in strange languages and laughed; and it was assumed that when they laughed, it was because the angels were reminiscing about their time on earth.

Sometimes they even shook hands.

While all this was going on, Prophet Khumalo stood up, singing 'Osana'. He was singing fast and furiously, occasionally breaking into strange tongues.

'We've descended upon you briefly,' he said in Shona, his right foot crooked, his body bent forward a little. He was standing facing the door. All prophets had graduated in various Vangwato church schools specialising in prophecy; Prophet Khumalo had graduated in teaching. Chidzidzisi.

'Can you please stand up for me, my son,' he said to Grandfather SaTimoty in Shona. Pastor Tshuma explained the instruction in Ndebele for the benefit of those who did not understand Shona.

The teaching by vadzidzisi had been a fascination for Mlungisi before he went to South Africa. But now it meant nothing. He did not believe the half of it. Seated with his head balanced in his arms, and watching as Prophet Khumalo spoke gravely, his mind strayed. For a moment he envisaged his younger brother, Given, smiling. And that image was soon replaced by that of his father, seated near the fireplace in the mud kitchen, shaving his head of white hair and reprimanding his now dead brother, Adam, about why he continued to live with 'bad people.'

He dozed off a little. And when he awoke, Prophet Khumalo was still teaching in Shona and Pastor Tshuma was still translating. He thought once more of the day he first arrived in South Africa, how the man who had transported him there had disrespected the traffic cops and how this had led to them ask about him: 'Does this passenger of yours have papers?' He'd been terrified, but they'd left him alone. Later his transporter told him that they were only trying to scare him, arresting illegal immigrants was not in their jurisdiction.

And then a few days later, his transporter took him to his mother in Alexander but she said she only had a quarter of what the transporter charged. And he'd left angry and promising to return for the rest. But his mother had changed her phone number. That had been a decade ago. Four years later, Mlungisi had paid the transporter the full amount out of his own pocket.

He thought about the dark ugly man with a beautiful wife who'd initiated him into the carpet cleaning business, telling him that this is where the ambitious succeeded. And how he'd worked very hard knowing what he wanted. And when he'd saved a considerable amount, inspired by the Lesotho immigrants, he'd bought an old van to collect scrap and done well in that business. The money had been helpful in covering some university expenses. Now, he rented out his old badly battered van for extra cash.

In a few months, he would get his degree; then he would hunt for a job, and when he found one, he would work and have money, buy a fancy car and a fancy house in Jo'burg; he'd then build a homestead in Malaba village, near his grandfather's, just so that people would not think that the city had turned him from his roots.

He knew some people would ask why he would not build a home in Kezi, near his father, but he determined to shut his ears. He and his father, who was now very old, would never get along. No, his rural home would consist of a single triple-storied house and it would house his wife; she would be a village girl. He would not choose a South African wife. No, he would never do anything to complicate his life, however rich he might become. He would live in the city, but he would come home frequently, not annually like some of the uncles he despised. And he would make sure his wife visited him regularly.

After daydreaming for what felt like hours, Mlungisi began to doze off. He was awakened by shuffling feet, people were getting up. It was the time for casting off the evil spirits, he realised this when he saw congregants arranging themselves to form a circle.

The congregants were talking about mundane things in whispers, joking, and a row between Tshuma and Dawu was going on – the former complaining that Dawu let the older children go to bed during the service, which was unacceptable.

A circle was quickly formed, with the women standing to the east, and the men to the west. Two pregnant young women knelt inside the circle, and then Pastor Tshuma and Pastor Joshua detached themselves from other men, laid their hands on the kneeling women's heads and prayed on their behalf, shouting loudly: their incoherent voices outdoing the song.

'I saw a clay pot filled with blood hidden somewhere in this home,' Prophet Zuma, of Gohole, said when the song ended and the woman had risen. 'And then I asked Jehovah what that meant, and he said to me, the blood in this pot is poison given little by little to the people of this house. There will be deaths, it could be children, it could be elderly people, but death is coming into this home, and one by one, the people of this homestead will go. Do you hear me, SaTimoty?'

'Hallelujah,' SaTimoty raised his eyes to the skies.

Then Prophet Zuma asked one of the pregnant women to listen carefully. He had a vision concerning her.

'I have been shown,' he said, 'a dark shadow following you. And I asked Jehovah what this shadow represented, and the Lord said 'Evil'. There is evil following you, hell-bent on making your life hard, young woman. Do you hear me?'

'Yes,' said the young woman.

'The evil following you is so strong you might lose everything you hold dear young woman, your baby, your marriage, everything. Do you hear me, *bazalwane*?'

'Hallelujah!' shouted the congregants.

MaNdlovu, SaEdwardi's wife, hastily began a song, and people sang along, making the hut boom. Then some young men with second sight jumped up and down, making strange noises in ancient tongues. A fast, serious song had that effect.

And then, quite expectedly, MaMoyo, aka Stumbana, a squat woman from Zintabeni, for whom everyone felt pity because she was ugly and poor and worked as a maid for poor people, even in her old age, was forcefully shoved into the circle by a young man called Patson. He made her kneel down and started to pray over her, singing very loudly, turning around her, and hitting her with the flaps of his bulky white wrap-around which he'd removed. And then Patson fell dramatically into the circle, men caught him. Some held his thrashing hands, others his kicking legs. It was presumed, he'd gotten himself possessed by the demon that had had previously been inhabiting MaMoyo, as he cast it out of her.

He continued writhing, trying to free himself from the men who restrained him. Mlungisi stood, watching, his thoughts whirling. He had grown up seeing so much of this, overwhelmed by the supernatural. But now he could hardly connect, or feel anything, except sympathy for the people who showed so much commitment to this sect.

'Who are you?' Tshuma asked the demon in Patson when he had been made to sit down and a white wrap-around had been tied around his neck.

'Uhmmm,' the demon said, wriggling, trying to free itself. It was well known that demons did not immediately answer. And Mlungisi remembered that some needed to be begged to respond. And how people had been critical of Pastor Tshuma's interrogative style, which yielded so little information. But Pastor Tshuma would not back off as he loved to insult demons and boast of having asked them baffling questions.

He continued shouting, 'Who are you?' and occasionally asking people to burn it with a song, during which time Patson, the possessed man, wriggled and writhed, attempting to free himself, and the demon, speaking through him, continuously cried out: 'I'm burning! I'm burning!'

'Who are you?' Pastor Tshuma asked after ordering a pause to the song.

'I'm Mtshakazi,' the demon said.

'Mtshakazi? Mtshakazi who?'

The demon said that it had offered enough information and demanded that it be allowed to stay. It won't do any harm, it promised. Tshuma pressed for more information but it refused. Then he ordered the song, and the demon began to speak begging that it be not burnt.

'Stop the song,' Tshuma ordered. 'Now speak! What is she to you?'

'I'm her grandmother,' said the demon.

'And what do you want with her?'

The demon said that it just wanted residence in her, nothing more. But when Tshuma accused it of lying and ordered a fast song to burn it, it cried out, saying it that was responsible for the harshness in Ma-Moyo's life, but willing to stop doing so, if it was not cast out.

19

'You're a filthy little demon, full of wanton vile, so I say burn burn burn and then leave her for good, she is not yours,' Pastor Tshuma screamed, while the congregants sang to burn the demon. After several bouts of wriggling, writhing, and groaning, Patson went limp and began to speak in ancient tongues. That meant the demon had left. It had been cast out.

A woman at the back started a song as the people returned to their original sitting positions, and when the song ended, Pastor Tshuma was the only one standing.

'Peace be with everyone,' he said.

'Amen,' the people said.

Walking about, rubbing his hands together, his eyes roving between the elderly woman at the back and the men around him, he asked if anyone else had something to say before he ended the service. Nobody responded.

'Then in that case, *bazalwane*,' he said, 'the service is over and you are dismissed.'

Dawu stood up at once and said something about how hungry she was.

'Tea,' she said. 'Tea, tea, tea.'

'Is needed,' echoed several young men from Bidi unashamedly. And that way, it was agreed that young women should go and make tea for everyone.

Tshuma asked who had a watch. What time it was.

'It's past four,' Mlungisi said, looking at his cellphone.

A paraffin lamp had replaced the fire in the hut. The hearth held only a single large coal buried in the ashes. Manto and Tamara brought some wood from outside and rekindled the fire, and soon the men huddled around the hearth.

Outside it was very cold and dark, the moon had set. The young women soon filled the kitchen to prepare tea. Mlungisi noticed a large fire when he went outside with Pastor Tshuma for a chat.

In the rondavel, excited conversations went on as people felt a release of tension. The young men from Bidi were talented in cracking jokes, not minding taking a swipe at anybody, as long as that somebody was not present.

One young man from Bidi said that he would sooner worship his cattle than that South African bishop, who was he, by the way? He had forgotten his name: the one who called his church Nazareth and his followers Nazarethans, when they were actually poor South Africans living in shacks.

Everyone laughed, and someone said that black people will never stop copying the ways of other nations.

Then SaTimoty, in his slow screechy voice, explained that when the Vangwatos' property had been reclaimed from the white man, all these lost people will realise that there is only one valid church: Vangwato. And they would join in droves. No comment was needed as it was a well-known fact.

Mlungisi began to feel both sleepy and bored. He longed to be back in Jo'burg, as if here, he was in the wrong place. And when she saw him drowsing, Grandmother NaTimoty took him to her house and prepared him a bed. 'See you in the morning,' she said when she was done, closing the door behind her.

There was a smell in his grandmother's house that deprived him of sleep. It was probably from the many bags of unwashed old clothes that filled the house, stacked on top of old wooden benches. He could not sleep now that he was in bed, but kept thinking of the events of the day, from when he'd left Harare in the morning. He began to dread a long boring day ahead. He would perhaps spend it resting in bed or sitting alone, thinking. And then at last on Sunday morning, he, his sister and Abraham would leave for Johannesburg. It seemed a long way off. He felt sad that after all, he'd not been able to find the right woman.

# The Woman

The sun was down when the woman returned home tired from a long journey peddling goods in distant villages. Before cooking supper she made herself a cup of tea and joined her husband, who sat on the veranda of their front house, carving. Her back had started to sting because of the sun, the load and the distance she'd travelled, but also from the welts remaining after the whipping her husband had given her on the previous night. She repeatedly felt the urge to touch them, but restrained herself because she did not want her husband to notice she was in pain. He was seated on a small wooden stool carving a club out of mopani wood. He was a short stout man with a very flat nose in a round face and a black stubble. He was working with concentration on his carving, holding the hatchet in his right hand, the wood in his left hand balanced over an old dish that was set upside down on the mud floor.

'The sun nowadays sets faster,' the woman observed. He did not respond.

'I mean,' the woman continued, 'I'd only reached Shizi and Isaka villages when I checked the clock and it said four. I was planning on going to Mashe.

'Winter is starting,' the man grunted.

'Do you want some… or?' she gestured to her cup of tea.

'No,' the man said. 'I'll have it at the usual time.'

'I'd have wanted it then, too,' the woman said. 'It's just that I'm hungry and tired.'

'It's been very hot today,' the man stated.

He continued working, and when he paused, he brushed off the wooden chips, which had accumulated in the dish, using his right boot. He looked up at the woman, and said, 'Did they buy?'

'Here and there. What can I say?'

The man did not say anything more for some time, and the woman continued to sip her tea. Neither were much given to talking and so they sat there, one drinking her tea, the other carving. When he was not watching, the woman furtively put her hand behind her back and felt the welts.

'How exactly did it go?' the man stopped carving.

'They only took five brooms on credit. They didn't even look at the pillows. It's bad when the month is this far advanced.'

They were quiet for a little while and then the woman continued, 'I'm only concerned about tomorrow. The mealie-meal will be finished today.'

The man stopped working and looked at her. 'Total total total?'

'Total,' the woman echoed.

He sat there thinking, holding the wood over the dish and the hatchet ready.

'World Vision will arrive on the 26th,' the woman said.

'I know,' the man answered, 'That's why I'm worried.'

'I could borrow a hundred from old Abraham and buy a twenty. His daughters send a thousand two hundred every month.'

'I don't like begging.'

'But we have no choice,' the woman said. 'Abraham and his wife aren't bad people.'

'I know,' the man said. 'But still I've never liked begging.'

He rose and disappeared into the house. It was a single-roomed dwelling built with red bricks. They used it as a bedroom and for storage, especially for food. The floor was baked mud polished with cow dung. The bottom of the plank door was half eaten away by termites and the single frame window was covered with flattened brown cardboard boxes held to the frame with wire. There was only a plank bed in one corner and a large sack on top of a chair in which they kept their clothes. The man brought out a small piece of glass, which he used to smooth the stick of his club.

'You were going to see NaMusa when I left earlier today,' the woman said when he was seated.

'That Satan of a woman does not want to pay me and I'm done with her,' he said. 'Next time she brings her pots here, I tell you, I'll direct her to Mpostoli.'

There was no more conversation until the woman finished her tea and stood up with her cup. She made a friendly comment about events in the village as she returned to the kitchen. The sun was now a big orange circle just above the horizon. The sky was still blue and cloudless, but a cold evening breeze had begun to set in.

In the kitchen, the woman first rekindled the fire by adding a few mopane sticks and blowing. Then she took one of the white aluminium pots from a built-in mud cupboard, half filled it with water, placed it on the iron pot-stand and sat down on a goatskin rug beside the fire, cutting spinach while waiting for the water to boil. The roofless kitchen had a hearth at the centre, nothing more. The floor, as in the house, was dark mud occasionally polished with cow dung. But it was starting to fade because she hadn't polished it for a long time. She was a very clean woman and she was always embarrassed when a visitor saw the floor so grey; she wished she had more time to devote to household chores but that could never be what with all the peddling and credit collecting she had to do to put food on the table for herself and her husband.

When the water boiled she went to fetch the mealie-meal. Food was stored in the front house because it was safer. The kitchen's plank door was so old and weak even chickens could break in. She cooked the sadza on the pot stand, the spinach under it on the coals, and when the sadza was almost ready, she took it off the stove and switched its place with that of the vegetable.

It was dark when she finished cooking and called her husband for supper. She found him standing and fiddling with the wooden poles that held the barbed wire. With a curtsey, she told him that food was ready. While cooking, she had thought of going to see NaMangwe, her neighbour, to hear more news about Ncube's daughter who was reported to have returned from a failed marriage with three children, but she decided against it. She would see her on the following day.

She fetched her husband's chair from the veranda, and carried it to the front of the kitchen. Then she brought the food over to him.

'I was talking to SaStodlana today,' he said while they were eating.

'Yes.'

He was quiet for some time, chewing patiently, as if he'd forgotten that he'd started a conversation.

'You went to see SaStodlana today,' she urged him to continue.

'I went to see SaStodlana today ... It's sad what's happening in Bulawayo. His two sons who live in Cowdray Park are back with all their children.'

'Some say the Operation will spill into the countryside.'

'We cannot know,' he said, chewing.

'But the senator's houses cannot be destroyed, surely. I mean, do you think they'll be destroyed if the Operation spills to the countryside?'

'You're asking me whether the senator's houses will be destroyed if the Operation extends here? How could I know?' the man said. 'Pass me the salt.'

The woman disappeared into the kitchen and returned with a small tin of salt which she handed to her husband with both hands.

'As I was saying ... it's very sad. I saw them, SaStodlana's sons and their children. It's very sad.'

'It is,' the woman said.

'They weren't a happy picture,' the man shook his head.

They continued talking about the Operation while eating, wondering if it would reach their village, and naming village business people with what they thought were illegal buildings that would be demolished. The woman did not stop feeling her back when she thought the man was not watching. But he'd noticed and he kept looking at her and shaking his head with disapproval.

'Hey, why didn't you use vinegar?' he finally snapped, when he couldn't take it anymore.

'What?' the woman asked, looking at him.

'You think I don't see you? Why didn't you use the vinegar?'

The woman said nothing.

'Use the vinegar and get over that stupid business of feeling your back.'

Again she remained silent but she determined to do as he advised that very night. She reproached herself for not having thought of it sooner.

'I'll find a fine sponge and apply it before we go to sleep', she said, before remembering that there was no vinegar.

They were quiet for a while, the man tapping the ground with his club, and the woman thinking about what lay ahead and the following day's chores. Then they started gossiping about their neighbours, how fat so-and-so's son was now; the news of the release of SaEster, a man who'd been imprisoned for stealing cattle, and the woman exclaimed in surprise and asked how he thought this SaEster would react to the rumours that his wife had been having an affair while he was in prison.

'Don't believe everything people say', the man advised her.

It was when the woman was washing the dishes and the man smoking and tapping the ground with the tip of his walking stick that a slight conflict began. The woman had made a careless remark saying she wished she had a putsununu who helped her with dishes. The man did not immediately burst out but when the woman repeated her words, saying she often envied NaMangwe, her neighbour, who would make her daughters wash the dishes while she rested, the man interpreted her words as a way of intimating that it was wrong of him to forbid her child to come and stay with them. The woman's son, she'd had by her first lover (who broke her heart), lived with the woman's parents in Gwanda.

'Shut up!' the man burst out angrily. He did not like to hear her talk that way. He'd warned her not to mention the issue but sometimes she alluded to it without knowing that she was doing so.

'Oh, I'm sorry Baba', the woman said. She did not like to upset him but sometimes he became upset over matters she didn't think would upset him. His temperament was very unpredictable. She'd unsuccessfully tried to master it in the fourteen years they'd spent together.

'No, you're not sorry,' he said now. 'You brought it up deliberately. You think I'll feel pity and let you bring that big-headed child of yours here to become a nuisance. Well, I won't. Forget it. If you want to be with him, the way to your own people is always open.'

'I'm sorry, Baba' she said again. It made her very sad to hear him refer to her son as a big-head. But she said nothing and pretended it didn't matter; indeed, the only thing that mattered was cooling his anger. At the start of their marriage he'd allowed the boy to stay with them, but one day, at the age of five, the boy broke a neighbour's window with a plastic ball while he was playing with friends and that was that. He was now seventeen.

'I'm sorry, Mpofu Baba, I didn't mean to…'

'No, shut up,' the man said.

They were silent for a long time as the woman continued washing the dishes, and placing them carefully in the mud cupboard above the tea-cups. She was busy trying to think what she could do to calm him down and make him forget what she'd said. When she was finished with dishes, the water in the aluminium bucket on the pot stand was singing and she came and knelt before him and asked, 'Would you want your tea before bathing or should I prepare you a bath first?'

'Make me tea first,' the man said.

The woman went back into the kitchen, scurried about, and then came out with a cup of tea on a saucer. She knelt down on the floor as she handed it to him.

He drank the tea quietly, only the pfff noise of his blowing at it, audible. When he'd finished, he handed the cup back to her and she washed it and returned it to the kitchen. Afterwards, she went to pour him bathing water at the front house and came to tell him that his bath was ready.

He remained seated as if he hadn't heard her though he had and the woman thought it wise to tell him again because if the water cooled, it was going to be her responsibility to heat it up again. 'The water will cool down,' she said.

'I'm sorry about snapping at you like that,' he said. 'It's just that…'I shouldn't have said what I said. I'm sorry,' the woman volunteered.

She was a very good woman and she liked peace and good fellow-ship but sometimes it was out of her power to achieve it. Her mother had recently died. And she'd heard that her father had lost his sight due to old age. She knew that her unmarried sister took care of her son at home, but sometimes she wished to be there for him. She also liked house music, but she had no access to it and she'd taught her-self to accept that you cannot have everything that you want.

'I'm also sorry about hitting you last night, I'm sorry. It will never happen again, it's just that ... you know ...'

'I crossed the line,' the woman said. 'You made it clear that you don't want a woman who comes home after dusk. I shouldn't have let NaPhumuzile keep me. I'm sorry too.'

'Your water is getting cold.'

'You know, you're a very good woman. I shouldn't be losing my temper like this.'

'It's a man's job to keep their woman in line,' she said. That is what she'd been taught, that men had the right to whip their women now and then, so when the pain from the beating had subsided, she took pride in these whippings, glad he was still beating her, contrary to those men she knew and despised, who used no whip but chased their woman away for the slightest misdemeanor.

He did not say anything for a while, but when he raised his head, he said, 'I'm still saddened by what befell SaStodlana's boys. Do you think the Operation will spill into the village?'

'I can't imagine the senator's buildings being demolished,' she said.

'About bathing, I'll do that tomorrow. I'm tired now. And besides, I didn't do anything hard today. I didn't sweat.'

Then they were quiet for some time and the woman disappeared in the kitchen and shortly came out, sat down on her hide rug and said, 'Tomorrow I'll be washing blankets. I was hoping you could borrow Ncube's bicycle so I could rush and buy a bar of soap at the store.'

'If he'll not be using it,' the man said. Then after a pause, he said, 'Why don't you use that money to buy mealie-meal. I mean, you know ...'

It's not enough,' the woman said.

'I hate begging,' the man said.

## The Woman

The woman sat thinking. After a long while, she noticed that her husband was drowsing in his chair. She scurried to the house and discarded the water she had prepared for his bath, before preparing him a bed. When she was done, she came and knelt before him and told him that the bed was ready She put his stool in the kitchen and pulled the door shut as he sauntered to the bedroom.

# Zedeck's Estrangement

They had planned to begin digging the well on Friday, but that Friday Zedeck arrived, and the work was consequently postponed indefinitely.

He was their son who had left home thirty years ago.

Looking at him closely, his mother, whose eyesight was still good, saw that his cheeks were sunken, his lips parched, his black tekkies were old and his denim jeans tattered. In short, nothing about him lived up to the usual grand elegance of those returning from the City of Gold. He might as well be returning from Gatsane Mine.

Over the following weeks, neighbours trooped to see him. The elderly among them, those who had known him before he left for South Africa, shook their gaunt heads, rolled their brown eyes, and whispered, 'is it really he?'.

Because he had brought nothing with him, not even a single pair of trousers to replace the ones he was wearing on his arrival, speculations were rife about the reason for his homecoming.

Some said that he'd been deported from South Africa and was ashamed to admit it, while others thought that maybe he was ill and had come home to breathe his last.

There was no corroboration or rebuttal, because Zedeck said nothing about himself, not even when drunk. He soon found a friend, Walter, who picked him up every morning and took him to the bottle store where they got drunk, before returning home in the evening.

After two months, his uncle, SaChipo, who lived in Plumtree district, arrived. He was the only living sibling of his father's, and had been volunteering at the church farm when he heard the news of Zedeck's homecoming.

He arrived toting a briefcase with the clothes and blankets he'd been using at the farm. He planned to stay a long while because he'd promised his brother, SaZedeck, that he was going to help him dig the well; Zedeck's homecoming had given him another reason to stay longer. Besides, he lived alone in Plumtree having lost his young wife to a *malayisha,* many years ago.

They had evening tea and supper with him, and just as the sun hung low over the trees that obscured the west horizon, SaZedeck took his brother to the field meaning to show him the site he'd chosen for the well, and the progress they'd made planting maize. They walked at the ends of ploughed land talking about too much rain and its disadvantages and, as they returned, SaZedeck took the opportunity to explain to SaChipo what he termed Zedeck's eccentricities.

He told him about his son's disinclination to bath or talk about his life in Johannesburg; his shirking and excessive drinking, and how he'd returned home dirty, drunk and empty handed like a beggar returning from street life.

'He goes drinking the whole day and comes home only to eat and sleep,' SaZedeck said, arms folded across his chest. 'It's as if he doesn't know or care who we are, it's as if he's lost all our values, and there is an air of mystery about him. You wouldn't believe he's the child we raised. Why, his mother and I have tried to arrange prayer services for him but he laughs the possibility off.'

Continuing, SaZedeck told his brother about the gloomy shadow overhanging his homestead, of the spirits that lurked and became active at night, causing all the life-long misfortunes which had interminably haunted his family.

'I'm dying,' he said. 'Any time from now I shall fall down and die. Not to say I have a serious illness. I just can feel death approaching. I can feel it in my bones. It won't have me lying in a bed first, no, it will

31

steal me while I'm on my feet. A very shameful way to die.'

And listening rapt, SaChipo felt very keen to help his brother in any way he could.

\*\*\*

His parents were old. SaZedeck had been strong when the young man left for Jo'burg thirty years ago, capable, indeed, of cycling the hundred kilometres to Bulawayo carrying a fifty kg sack of maize on his bicycle. Now, he was frail, dependent on the meagre seasonal harvests from his two fields and on his scattered sons and daughters, particularly Albert who did very well gold panning at Turk Mine. SaZedeck and his wife were devout Protestants, and they believed their son's arrival was a response to their prayers, God's work. All they were living for now was to peacefully depart from this earth, and enter a new one, as described in the bibles they read and lived by.

They'd been married for more than five decades, and had had more than fifteen children, four of whom had died and came only as corpses for them to bury. The others were scattered across the world, but kept in touch. Zedeck was the only one they hadn't known anything about, until he'd pitched up looking like a vagabond.

When drunk, Zedeck asked after the people he'd known before he went south, and would grimace as he learned their fates. But he would affect a charming persona when asking after his female age mates, which led everyone to suspect that he'd dated them.

He was a man with extreme ambitions, who didn't see meaning in a life of unfulfilled dreams. Born into poverty during the colonial rule, he'd been forced to fight for freedom as a child, freedom won but quickly lost. Then he'd been forced out of his country, he and other child-freedom fighters, by poverty and persecution. Being ambitious, he'd spent many years trying to turn his life around. Hired here and there, working in the sweltering sun; confident, despite the odds, that he would make it large in life. He had imagined himself rich with the world at his fingertips coming home only to flaunt his wealth and show largesse. He'd had the energy and the will; hatred of poverty fuelled his efforts. But again and again, undocumented in a foreign country, his efforts had gone to waste. Failure had tormented his soul and he felt like a fish in a frying pan, knowing he would die without becoming the person he'd imagined. With no more dreams, the only thing that kept him moving was freedom, freedom from everyone and everything.

Home had given him what he was looking for, indeed more than he'd expected. He had no children, and he saw it as an advantage, though he had once wanted them. When drunk, he spoke a lot to keep his mind busy. The beer afforded him that.

'*Kudliwani laph' ekhaya?*' he wagged his small head though he'd he wasn't hungry when MaDube served dinner earlier.

MaDube went to fetch his food from her house and served him on a small round table, a bowl of okra and of sadza. He washed his hands in a small metal dish, but did not bother to dry them with the napkin provided. With his right hand, he scooped the sadza from its bowl and put it together with okra. He then placed the bowl on his lap and began eating greedily.

A high-pitched jackal's laughter was heard from outside.

His father said, 'Bloody beasts. They eat my goats.'

'A neighbour of mine lost three goats in one night,' SaChipo added.

Food in his mouth, Zedeck announced in a loud voice that in the morning he and his friend Walter went to check on Mbiko's cattle at the Shashe ranch, and had had a good time. (Mbiko was the owner of the bottle store from which he drank.)

Nobody commented.

Zedeck, who was feeling energetic, continued, his mouth full. 'One of these days you'll be surprised to wake up and find both fields weeded from end to end'.

'You can't even weed a square metre. How will you weed a field?' his mother asked laughing.

He ignored the question, asking instead if Hloniphani, the cripple who used to roam the village on a wheel chair, was still alive? Still working at the Khulumusenza Grinding Mill?

'Hloniphani died a very long time ago,' his mother answered him.

Whether he heard the answer or not, no one could tell. Because just then, he announced that one of these days, he would go to Khulumusenza. Maybe he'd meet an old friend who'd buy him a beer.

And then, without a pause, he asked why Albert was working at Turk Mine when there were plenty of mines nearby. But before anyone could answer, he went on to tell them how nice it always was at the bottle store, and how well his friends danced, though he himself, didn't.

No one replied.

'Walter is a great man,' he continued.

Silence.

'He's a remarkable person.'

Again they ignored his remarks which to them seemed pointless.

After supper SaChipo and SaZedeck talked about the church farm, marvelling at the developments, and how even during the dry season, the crops never failed; God worked, they agreed. They talked more about the well they were planning to dig in the field, how Mbobho, the neighbour who forbade them to fetch water from his, would be envious after they had dug theirs.

'The women will have to plant lots of vegetables,' SaZedeck said, swigging water from a huge jug. He picked his stool up and placed it near the door, pushing it a little wider for fresh air.

SaChipo unzipped his sweater and tied it around his waist, minutes later, he took it off again and put it on the floor, fanning himself as he did so.

He'd had a great time at the church farm, SaZedeck continued, the food was good and plentiful. And there were many people all volunteering without shirking. A young man called Mdawini had given him a phone; he took it out of his blazer pocket and showed it around – an old twentieth century Nokia.

And then at nine, before they went to bed, they prayed. They knelt on the floor, facing the east, wearing white drapes. Zedeck went outside and roamed the courtyard, smoking. He never participated. He didn't see the point.

Tuesday morning was humid. Large grey cumulus clouds appeared on the horizon. Towards the afternoon the rain threatened but strong winds drove the clouds away. Work in the field was lighter, owing to SaChipo's presence. He controlled the plough while SaZedeck carried the whip and MaDube sowed. NaZedeck weeded the groundnuts in their rows at the back of the field. Zedeck went to the bottle store.

And then on Wednesday, when SaZedeck and SaChipo had planned to talk to Mpofu about digging the well, there was rain. It poured from dawn until late in the afternoon, leaving behind pools of water which took a long time to dry because the ground was saturated. Finally, the two old men went to see Mpofu on Wednesday the following week. He agreed to help them, but SaChipo thought he was charging too much.

'Six times fifty kg of maize is three hundred kg and that isn't a trifle,' he snorted on their way back.

'And we'll be working with him,' SaZedeck added.

Work on the well began on the Friday. First, they uprooted a small mopane tree, and weeded and fenced the perimeter of the area with slim mopane trunks.

'The women will have to plant lots of vegetables,' SaZedeck reiterated throughout the day.

The digging started on a Sunday morning. Mpofu brought many tools, some of which he had cycled to borrow from his brother in Mambale. SaZedeck made a *lima,* inviting those neighbours he was in good standing with to help. The men worked until their backs would not allow them to stand upright. MaDube and NaZedeck cooked plenty of food and served it, with the help of a girl from next door. Working men preferred beer but SaZedeck as a church man forbade the drinking of beer in his homestead, and served them *amahewu.* By evening a large mound of dark, gravelly clay sat beside a very deep ditch. But the depth was still short because they hadn't caught the vein of water.

On the following days, Mpofu mostly worked alone, SaZedeck and SaChipo joining him in the evenings after working in the field. He was working patiently.

Zedeck did not participate in the digging of the well, as he didn't in anything else. When he felt like it, he strode to the site of the well at the back of the field, and stood hands in the pockets of his old jeans given him by MaDube, watching as Mpofu worked. Sometimes he would ask for the pick, and dig in quick short bursts, only to give the implement back to Mpofu before achieving anything of substance, panting like an old horse. Mostly, he didn't even wander near the site of the well.

On the morning of the Thursday that lightning killed a child in a nearby village, SaChipo caught him just as he went out the gate, heading for the bottle store. The sun was sweltering. He walked side by side with him, down the rutted footpath, telling him what he thought he needed to know. That his parents expected him to participate in household chores. For example, he could mend the fence of the field, or help with the weeding, or find a job as a night watchman at the shops. Nobody expected too much from him. Just a little so the strain of a handless mouth was not felt by others.

Zedeck remained apathetic, and SaChipo decided to exert more pressure by nagging him at every opportunity – in the mornings before he left for the bottle store and in the evenings when he came home drunk or pretending to be drunk.

'Everyone is worried about you,' he would say. 'You can rebuild your life.'

The rain affected him. And on the days when a persistent rain prevented him from going to the bottle store, each minute dragged more sluggishly than the minutes before because his uncle would not shut his mouth. Confined together in the front hut, his uncle would reiterate that he should find work and then follow that by warning him against drinking. 'It's never been a solution,' he would say. 'You can bounce back. You can rebuild your life again.'

He did so on a cold Sunday; a small drizzle that had persisted throughout the night did not subside the whole day and kept everyone indoors. They were seated in the front hut, Zedeck, NaZedeck, SaZedeck and SaChipo, who had brought a Bible. MaDube was with the boys in the cooking shack, cooking *umxhanxa*.

'You can turn your life around,' SaZedeck said. 'Trust in the lord with all thine heart. And lean not unto thine own understanding.'

SaChipo looked up at Zedeck from the Bible, his small brown eyes searching Zedeck's: 'You've still got a long life ahead of you, son."

A large fire of *mtswiri* wood was burning, throwing sparks everywhere.

SaChipo followed that with a tirade about responsibility. Unable to bear his uncle's pestering, Zedeck quietly stood up and walked out, accidentally kicking a drenched rooster huddled at the door. He stayed out in the rain for the whole day and did not come to the kitchen for supper that evening. The children, sent to return a box iron borrowed from a neighbour, reported that they saw him walking pensively in the trees, his long-sleeved shirt soaked and his face dribbling with sweat; and he had squinted at them uninterestedly, as if he knew them not.

The conflict between uncle and nephew escalated. Sometimes at bedtime, his parents, whose bedroom was near the one SaChipo shared with Zedeck, heard the muffled arguments that usually lasted until they lost interest and slept.

'My life is my own business, Babomncane!' was Zedeck's usual retort. Sometimes these arguments were followed by the frenzied click of the keys on the padlock and in the morning, SaChipo would grunt that Zedeck had left at night, '...because he can't face the bloody truth!'

They gathered that what was so often crossly talked about was Zedeck's disinclination to bath. Out of politeness, SaChipo did not talk to his nephew about his unwillingness to wash in front of everyone else. Instead, he spoke to him at night, telling him that he smelt and dirtied the bedclothes, thus putting an additional strain on MaDube, who had to wash them.

Sometimes Zedeck simply stayed at Walter's until they quarreled. Months came and went. Zedeck remained unchanged, and SaChipo changed tactics.

'Nothing but evil spirits could make someone so obstinate, so sunk in bad ways,' he told his brother one morning while they sat in the front hut, having breakfast. 'We need an exorcist.'

And thus it was agreed that an exorcism would have to be performed on Zedeck. His parents told their son of their plans, and his apathy told its own story. He seemed indifferent to everything except alcohol.

They found the right exorcist in a prophet who lived in Maphisa called Gumbo. He was a member of their church, and had a good reputation. They called him on SaChipo's phone to check if he could visit them on a Saturday. He was available, and a deal was made.

'Maybe *singake siphumule*,' his mother said, hoping that exorcism would make a difference.

But on the Saturday, Zedeck was not to be found. Days passed, but still there was no sign of him. Nobody had seen him, not even Walter. He'd gone. And somehow his parents knew, intuitively, that this was forever.

That year, the rain was abundant. The earth was always sodden, and there were pools of water everywhere. There was so much water that drought-resistant crops like millet and sorghum suffered as if there'd been no rain at all. The well they were digging was always filled with water, and that was both an advantage and a disadvantage.

They planted more maize, and added wheat and rice in the swampy area near the amarula tree, an area they usually left uncultivated. They began to eat watermelons early, five weeks earlier than usual. Not seeing him, the neighbours assumed that SaZedeck's first-born son had returned to Johannesburg.

Years passed but his parents did not forget him. For years, they discussed their son, wondering what could have made him abandon them, so soon after their reunion. Occasionally, they concluded that it was the beer, but with time, they reasoned that it couldn't have been the beer, it was only a by-product. Nor was it his uncle's pestering.

The truth, of course, didn't come at once, it slowly became visible over a long time, as it morphed into form or fluttered into intuition. It was the dread of the ignominy of death after an empty life and the peculiar preference for dying alone, out of sight, that led their son to disappear so quickly; that had led him stay in Johannesburg unwilling to return home until deportation forced him back. It comforted them to think that he might still be alive, living off wild fruits in the mountains or begging in a town.

A fuss would be made, someone would cry, people would gather to bury them, stones would be erected, memories would be created. But none of that could happen to him. Zedeck would die, but no one would cry, no one would fuss, no one would make memories. No one has ever mourned the death of a vagrant.

What they knew for certain was that they were not going to bury him and he wasn't going to bury them, they were not going to mourn his death and neither was he going to mourn theirs. In death as in life, they would remain apart, he alone. No one would know his tomb. No one would know when and how his life ended.

For more years to come they would continue working in their fields, striving, managing, suffering and hoping. But then one by one they would eventually die. And people would make a fuss, mourn them, make memories, but none of that would happen to him. No one would mourn or remember him because no one ever mourned or remembered someone who never was.

# The Service

The congregation wanted someone with verve. That was the Binga prophet. He'd been invited but still had not arrived. So in the meantime Prophetess Dawu was in charge of the service. She stood near the fireplace singing.

Prophetess Dawu's failing lay in her lack of imagination. Every Saturday night she gave a single prophesy, and always the same one. The congregants had grown tired of it. They needed fresh prophecies, drama and theatrics. The Binga prophet always brought these in abundance.

Today the old lady tried many tricks: first she went about shaking awake the drowsing young men and women, and sprinkling cold water on them. Then she started making strange sounds. But nothing worked. The elderly people continued to sing as if they had plum stones hidden under their tongues. The young people continued drowsing as if they'd been on endless vigils. Prophetess Dawu finally sat down, depressed. Pastor Tshuma rose.

He was a tall, gaunt man with a tanned face.

'*Kufarira vangwato,*' he said.

He meant to dismiss the service but something stopped his mouth. Three men marched into the hut, a fat middle-aged one in the lead: the Binga prophet. And like a miracle, his mere arrival roused everybody.

The Binga prophet was a short, paunchy man with a long tubelike face; handsome though, thanks to his sharp nose and fixed smile. He was also a healer and an exorcist, and had healed many people and purged many an evil spirit in Malaba village. So he was idolised far and wide.

He sat down on the brown floor with his companions, but as soon as Pastor Tshuma did the same, he rose and began a slow, mournful song, which, nonetheless, he soon ended. Quickly, he gave his reasons for being late, which had something to do with his sick wife and imprisoned son. 'Even for us men of God things go awry sometimes,' he told us before demanding a hymn.

The deep voice of a young man in the middle row quickly provided it, and several of the youth rose and sang with ear-splitting voices, and evident new energy. As the song rose to a crescendo, the Binga prophet started pacing along the seated rows, starting with the youth and then the middle-aged women, where, for a few minutes he stood and stared out of a tiny window.

In the fireplace, the mtswiri wood burned with a purplish flame. Behind the grandmothers, the door gaped into the dark night like an open black mouth. The congregation occupied one side of the hut and sleeping children in old, threadbare blankets, the other. There were sixty or more worshippers. Some came from Matemani, some from St Josephs, others from Mzila, a few from Mazwi, most from Tshelanyemba, and a couple from Maphisa. They all came to praise the Lord, to ask him for protection from evil spirits, for security from untimely death, and supernatural love to give to their enemies. They wanted rains and boreholes, love and blessings, food and clothes and, above all, a place in the kingdom of heaven.

They sang songs asking God to empower Father: Father referring to their self-exiled church leader who lived in Lusaka. Some of their songs asked God to purge all evil spirits, while others merely requested blessings. Everyone raised their voices high, young men, young women, and even the grandmothers in the back row. Only a few, like Pastor Nyoni, croaked. He even remained seated while others stood because he suffered from sore knees that had tormented him for many years.

Smirking and nodding, the Binga prophet lifted both his hands to stop the current song. Again he paced through the seated rows, his arms outstretched before him, and paused beside the hearth, raised his sharp chin, and cast his brown eyes around. There was a complete silence, which he broke with an announcement that among them were devious elements colluding with witches outside the church in order to hamper the progress of the service.

'And,' he said, twisting his face, 'It is my duty to name and shame them. I'd do just that.'

Lip-trilling, he took off his white wrapper, folded it, and squeezed it into the window, originally intended as an air-vent. 'But before we get to that,' he said, turning from the window. 'We'll first heal the sick and rid this place of evil spirits.'

He had barely finished saying this when one of his companions, a lanky young man with a square head, started to sing 'Jomana'. Everyone, male and female, young and old, leapt to their feet and sang. The hut boomed with their voices which almost cracked the mud wall. The Binga prophet began leaping up and down, flapping his hands furiously as if he wanted to fly.

'They're retreating,' he announced some moments later, after stopping the song with his upraised palms. 'They're finally running back to their masters.'

'Now,' he continued, 'We're going to do miracles. Miracles that once existed in the past are now happening here in Africa with a few chosen people like you.'

He started walking to and from the door, rubbing his palms together, chanting and lip-trilling. 'Let's have a powerful song someone,' he said, pausing near the door.

His lanky companion with a square head began 'Jomana' again, singing heartily, so that towards the end of the song, the Binga prophet was now both nodding and skipping; this meant he was filled with the holy spirit and ready to purge evil spirits.

He started with demons. Aided by his companions, he cast the first one out of Mary, an ugly twelve-year-old girl from Mazwi. She had been raped thrice in her life, her father explained to the prophet. And the demon, speaking through the Binga prophet, claimed full responsibility for the young lady's strange appeal to lustful elderly men.

The Binga prophet then cast the second demon out of Washington, the worst pauper in Malaba village. And that demon too, speaking through the Binga prophet, claimed full responsibility for the pauper's unenviable social situation that, to those who knew, had tormented his clan over many generations.

The Binga prophet then began the hymn: 'Up in heaven are angels with Jehovah, only the purest will be received.' Men joined in with their bass voices while women provided the counterpoint.

Still leading the song, the Binga prophet went outside with the pastors to exorcise a goblin at the chickens' tree to the left of the front gate.

It was sent to hinder the proliferation of livestock, the prophet explained to the pastors after hitting the evil creature down and dead with a single flapping of his drape. Dead on the ground, the goblin resembled the plucked body of a crow. But in a grave tone, the Binga prophet explained that the malevolent creature could assume any form when alive, including that of a short, bearded white man, which was how it typically appeared to those who had the misfortune to see it alive with their natural eyes. The pastors gazed at the dead goblin, their hearts thumping with triumph. It was wrapped in different coloured wools, and had two feathers of a guinea fowl protruding from its supposed head like the ears of a hare.

The Binga prophet then gravely explained to pastor SaTimoty, as owner of the homestead, that the goblin's master was his neighbour who lived to the south of his homestead; an aging widow with failing eyes. Pastor SaTimoty nodded his head sagely, he recognised the woman instantly.

The Binga prophet exorcised another goblin at the front gate before they returned to the hut. After a few poignant songs, he started prophesying.

He directed his first vision towards a pretty, unmarried, middle-aged woman from Tshelanyemba. She'd loved too many men at one time, he told her, and that was the reason she still hadn't found Mr Right despite her age. Solution, he said, lay in prayer and also in her willingness to become a respectable woman who loved only one man at a time.

Next the Binga prophet prophesied that a pregnant woman from Matemani would have a miscarriage. Her too friendly near neighbour wanted to kill the baby. It was her turn to kill at a witch-club, and she'd targeted the unborn child because it was defenseless. She (the woman from Matemani) and her husband were not praying hard enough, that was the reason behind this.

A squat man from St Josephs followed: the Binga prophet told him that his closest neighbour and friend had planted the paw of a baboon in his sorghum field to make his crop fail. Secondly, he warned, one of his children would unexpectedly fall sick and die before the end of the year. It would be bewitched by the same neighbour and friend to make a goblin from the child's soul. Averting the catastrophe, the Binga prophet said, would, as always, be dependent on how hard the squat man prayed and fasted.

Many people followed. He told MaMoyo, a woman from Maphisa, to stop yearning for other men and show love to Sibanda, her husband. And a thirteen-year-old boy from Mazwi that his chest smelt of goats' hair and that he should stop sleeping with animals.

And finally, when many congregants had been helped, Pastor Nyoni came before the prophet. Pastor Nyoni was prophetess Dawu's husband. He had sore knees. When this was explained to the Binga prophet, the Binga prophet's lanky companion began a deep soulful hymn, which he and Pastor Nyoni sang as they circled the pastor.

'Do you know what happened to your knees Baba,' asked the Binga prophet, when the slow, sad song had ended, confusing Pastor Nyoni, who'd only expected answers. The old man stammered. One of the Binga prophet's companions started another lament while flapping their white wrap-arounds above his bald head. The song ended with the Binga prophet mumbling, sniffing and casting the whites of his eyes over the congregation.

'Now, Baba,' I asked you a question and you didn't answer me,' the Binga prophet persisted. 'I'll now repeat myself – do you know why your knees are sore?'

Pastor Nyoni looked about him with sad eyes, and then humbly stammered that he had no idea. Everyone was staring, curious eyes traversing the distance between the sick pastor and the prophet. The

Binga prophet then paced to the door behind the grandmothers, turned, and called out:

'Can you stand up for me, Mama Dawu?' He rubbed his hands fervently, while shaking his head.

Prophetess Dawu rose, and stood with her back to the Binga prophet. He then shuffled near the fireplace, and stood facing the two of them.

'He's your husband, right?'

She nodded.

'Can you please tell him why his knees are sore?'

There was a nervous, ominous silence, one which usually heralds a cataclysmic eruption. The Binga prophet then started pacing around the hearth, humming.

'Baba,' he said, standing with his head slightly tilted over his right shoulder. 'You're being used at night as a horse on a witch's errands. That is why your knees are sore. And if you've any questions regarding the purpose of these and all other trivialities,' he said, turning his eyes to Prophetess Dawu. 'This woman here has all the answers.'

It was like a thoroughly rehearsed theatre performance. No sooner were the words out the Binga prophet's mouth than Prophetess Dawu had swept to the front, and stood before Pastor SaTimoty, who sat with his legs stretched before him.

'SaTimoty,' she cried. 'What's all this, SaTimoty? Hhi, SaTimoty, what's this? You want to destroy my family? You invited these Binga people here to tell me that I'm a witch, and I ride my own husband? How can you do that, SaTimoty? Hhi, SaTimoty?'

There was fury in prophetess Dawu's voice, as she raved, the drama escalating: 'How long have I been attending church at your homestead, SaTimoty? Who have I ever bewitched? Then why have you invited these people here to say that I'm a witch? Where did I learn that witchcraft? Hhi, SaTimoty? You've a problem with me attending church here at your homestead? Okay, I'm leaving then. I'm leaving right now. I'm leaving and I won't ever come back.'

Pastor SaTimoty stared passively at her as if she was mad. She started rousing her grandchildren who were sleeping on rugs to one side of the hut, threatening to leave at that very hour, and never be seen again. But everyone knew that what she was doing or saying, despite her very real emotion, was just an expected, necessary reaction to the charges made against her. She was never going to leave, things were shortly going to return to normal, for such incidents at Vangwato church services were not uncommon. They were an entertainment. And despite the bad blood they invariably caused, the village worshippers needed them so as to have exciting things to think about, colourful memories to help them forget the emptiness in their lives: hence nobody was to blame. The Binga prophet was only fulfilling his duty as an entertainer, and doing what the congregation expected of him. It was what made him exciting and lovable. He had performed similar tricks in all churches to which he was invited, so as to maintain his reputation as a strong, charming, fearless prophet. The one in demand.

So while Prophetess Dawu was still fussing over what was really nothing, someone in the middle rows with a high-pitched voice began a song, and there was a deafening echo as everyone joined in; the service had just begun again, or so it felt to the worshippers.

# Beauty is in the Eye of the Beholder

SaElvis Nyoni is dead. He was ninety-five. I've just received that news from my mother. He was perhaps the most interesting person I've ever known. Not family, of course, but I knew him well because he was a member of our Protestant church – Bazalwane, where everyone knows everyone. I was no fan of his, I just found him interesting. Same way as I did Josiah, Sayizi, Themba, Mdolomba, Bra Thami and my own grandfather. Their lives intrigued me. Especially now that they're all dead.

Josiah was a healer and exorcist who slept with all his female patients. He enchanted them, slept with them, and then married them. He died at fifty-four from TB. Nine wives and twenty-seven children survived him.

Sayizi died after a short illness. Some say he was hit by goblins on the night he left his wife to visit a girlfriend. It was well known he loved women too much. Some say he died because his father, SaSarafira, rejected everyone's advice that he should consult a witchdoctor; but he was a very devout Bazalwane member, and we consider witchdoctors ungodly.

Themba never lived with one woman in one place; never started out with a woman. Never, except when he was a young man. He was a drifter, and a powerful singer with an angelic voice. He boasted that no widow ever kept him for more than two years. He died not very long ago. What everyone remembers him about is his love

47

for widows, his drifting, and the song: 'Beyond the city of Bulawayo there is God,' which he'd composed himself.

Mdolomba was a rapist. He raped old women, young school children, and even boys. He lived his life on the run. He broke out of prison twice and finally gunned himself down when the police were about to capture him for the third time. It was sad because those who knew him before he turned to crime said he was a great singer, pianist and dancer, and had squandered such beautiful talents.

Bra Thami survived on beer which was not allowed at Bazalwane, but he drank it anyway. He was a war veteran, and had gone to Zambia, then Canada and had returned home after nineteen years in exile, a hero and a celebrity in the village. He earned both war veteran and disability pensions, which made him one of the highest paid people in Buturura. His friends say at month-end, he would wake you at six a.m. and pay you to accompany him to the money machine, where he would withdraw all his salary and buy beers with the half of it. When he had money, he would offer to buy strangers whatever their hearts desired. He finally died from cancer while staying with MaMhlophe of Silawa who had managed to get him to quit drinking.

Yet, of all these men, SaElvis intrigued me the most. The best way to describe him is that he was simultaneously a lover and a hater. As an old man he loved young women and wanted to marry them all while hating my grandfather who was notorious for thwarting marriages. He once used his powers as the most senior leader of our church to thwart SaElvis's marriage to Sakhile, a girl from next door. That sparked a lifelong feud. But their argument did not start there. It had begun years before when my grandfather thwarted a marriage between one of my uncles and SaElvis's daughter Letiwe. She had come to my grandfather's so that he could pray for her. In the course of her stay, Uncle Bernard impregnated her. Then he wanted to marry her, but my grandfather said no, Letiwe could not be his daughter-in-law, she had no manners; and that was it. SaElvis went mad.

Averting marriages was my grandfather's business. He once foiled a marriage between Uncle Michael and a Maphisa girl called Tsepang. This sparked a deadly feud. One that culminated in Tsepang's father attempting to hit my grandfather with an axe. Tsepang was pregnant but my grandfather did not care. Perhaps it's the one thing that everyone remembers about my grandfather now that he's dead. That, and his devoutness. He also frustrated a marriage between another of my uncles and a neighbouring girl, simply because he suspected the girl's father of witchcraft. My uncle had sneaked the girl into the house to sleep with her, but my grandfather heard him. He announced that he'd dreamt that a snakelet had entered his homestead. The girl's father almost felled my grandfather with an axe when he heard about it.

The feud between my grandfather and SaElvis was the worst. It culminated when the latter poisoned my grandfather with a calabash of makheu. He lay in coma for three weeks, a pint of thick beer in his system.

SaElvis was a tricky man. There's an infamous story that he and his first wife plotted to kill his third wife. It's said that NaKhumbu, his third wife, had a minor headache when the two, SaElvis and his first wife, insisted on calling a prophet-healer to help her. And then they paid the man two cattle to put muthi in the water he used to cure her, and when NaKhumbu drank the water, she almost died.

He was the subject of many scandals. Once he broke up with fifteen-year-old Tania just a few months after the marriage. Soon afterwards, he'd tried to marry thirteen-year-old Sibusiso and failed because my grandfather foiled the marriage. He did not do so for moral reasons as some might believe. Many a time, he'd married my aunts off to men thrice their ages. My mother was fourteen when my grandfather married her off to my father who was fifty-nine. Aunt Thandiwe was twelve when she was given to the polygamist, Nduna, aged fifty-two. My grandfather's reasons for thwarting marriages were known only to himself. All we knew was that he both frustrated and arranged marriages.

The most enthralling of all of SaElvis's scandals, was that of an affair he had with an epileptic girl called Lucy. It is also a very painful story.

It was in July 1977 that Sebezile and Nkosi, a devout Bazalwane couple, entrusted their five-year-old daughter to SaElvis. He was to pray for her until the epilepsy was cured. It could take a lifetime, but that was no problem to anyone. Incidents of the sort were not uncommon. All Josiah's wives arrived that way. But SaElvis had no such history. He used to cure people and let them lead their own lives. He'd got all his three wives fair and square in the traditional way.

So, Lucy stayed with SaElvis, being looked after by Manyoni, his first wife; she never attended school, not even the first grade. She grew better over time, but then the fit, or the condition (we thought it was a disease), would start again, so for her to return to her parents was considered inexpedient.

Meantime, Lucy grew to become a most beautiful girl, praised by everyone for her looks; at the age of just eleven, a boy from Seula asked for her hand in marriage, but SaElvis, acting as her guardian, declined. It was understood. Her parents had no say, but they approved his actions; she would only get married when she was finally cured.

Of course, Charles, the Seula boy, was not the only one to covet such a beautiful young woman. Many a young man did. Patimile, Ngulube, and Joseph to name just a few. But they were all turned down: SaElvis citing Lucy's sickness.

The year was 1985 when Lucy's father died. He was forty-four. He was killed in a car accident. Months later, his wife followed him after a short illness. Lucy had become an orphan.

It was a few years after this that we heard rumours that Lucy, now fourteen was pregnant. By who? Nobody knew. She bore a girl. The father was never discovered. Only speculation suggested the child was SaElvis's. But who could confront him and demand the truth? Whether the child was really his or not was nobody's business.

Meanwhile, her sickness was said to have been finally cured. And Patimile, a young man from Mashumba – perhaps, because he was deaf, he felt he was entitled to Lucy, given that she too suffered from a disability – never stopped paying her court. But he too was refused by SaElvis, and everyone understood.

It was at this time that SaElvis plotted with his first wife to kill his third wife. The grudge he had with my grandfather was also settled around this time. Thembani, Uncle Bernard's son, the one he'd made with SaElvis's daughter, was now old enough to ask his grandfathers to bury the hatchet, saying their feud affected his life: he couldn't find a job, love, or happiness and according to the prophets he'd consulted this was because of their feud. Perhaps it was only a pretense, but the two old men reconciled.

It was also at this time, that Martha, the girl next door, went to see Josiah over recurring stomach pains. My grandmother warned her to be careful with Josiah. Some say Josiah used muthi to enchant women, and though I do not believe in muthi, I could offer this case as an exception. I remember the day, it was sunny. My grandmother was seated under a snot-apple tree in the field. I cannot remember what she was doing, but I remember Martha, all dressed up to meet Josiah in Sobukhwe, telling my grandmother, 'I'm going to see him tomorrow, Aunty.'

'I guess we don't need to tell you about Josiah,' my grandmother said sternly. 'You know about him yourself. Six of his wives went to him seeking help and ended up married to him. Just look at how they are suffering. I hope you will be wise enough not to let him trick you.'

And this is what Martha said; 'Oh, no, Aunty...' She called my grandmother Aunty, though she wasn't her aunt... 'You needn't worry about me. Soon as he tries to trick me, I'll make sure to scream and leave as soon as possible. I'm not that foolish girl, Aunty.'

But, guess what happened? She is now one of Josiah's widows, she has four children by him and she's only thirty-one now, as I write this story. He died when she was twenty-six.

However, Patimile never stopped paying court to Lucy. But he was consistently turned down and told that she still needed to be cured. Some say Lucy loved him and was hurt by SaElvis's objection to their marriage. They say that one day, when SaElvis had gone to the Bazalwane church elders' meetings with all his wives except Na-Khumbu, Lucy had tried to run to Patimile in Mashumba. This rumour is unsubstantiated, but I don't see why people would lie. They say that many a time, Lucy had cried and asked to be allowed to marry Patimile, but SaElvis, as her guardian with the duty to cure her of epilepsy, had consistently refused. Some people even allege hat Patimile had once accused SaElvis of unfairly hindering his and Lucy's love, but the church elders, who heard the matter, voted in favour of SaElvis, citing unforeseeable difficulties.

It was in the November of that year when we received news that Lucy was healed. I remember that because we were just starting to plant, and we usually began planting in November when the first rains fell. The news, or the rumours, was heard during one of the church parties attended by people from many areas. Everyone remained doubtful. But later we saw Lucy, more beautiful than ever, (she was pregnant at the time) and she confirmed the news herself. She had come for another of the big church parties which were held at my grandfather's because of his senior position in the church.

As with the first child, nobody knew officially who the father was though, in fact, it was a well-known secret. Moreover, SaElvis started accompanying her everywhere; he seemed to love her more than he loved his wives.

Other children were born – in no time, Lucy had seven children – and the speculations swelled. Some said the children were Patimile's but most people refuted that, and Patimile denied it. Still, he continued to pay court to Lucy. People pitied him, courting a woman with so many children who weren't his own. However, by then, because it was believed that Lucy was cured, Patimile was promised, a date for the wedding was given and postponed, given and postponed, and many years came to pass while this continued.

Mdolobha died. Josiah too. Bra Tami as well.

And then a sad thing happened. News reached us that Lucy had gone to fetch roofing sedge with Manyoni from Msoro Dam when she fell into a fire while left alone to prepare food. The fire had eaten half her body. I saw her a year later: the right side of her face was purple, is purple, I mean, because Lucy is still alive and if you go to Mashumba right now, you will see her for yourself. Her lips and her nose are nowhere. It's a miracle that she didn't die.

This marked an end to Lucy's remarkable beauty. With her mouth half gone, her face two different colours, no right ear just a piece of jutting flesh like a large pustule, according to some of us, no man could ever want her. But then, shortly after this, we heard news of

Lucy's forthcoming marriage to Patimile. The dates were set and the wedding happened. Lucy was finally married to deaf Patimile. He had no children and Lucy went to him with three of hers. Even, today, as I write their story, they're still together. Happily married. According to insiders, there is peace in their marriage: she doesn't like to argue with him and he doesn't like to argue with her, and when one makes a mistake, he or she apologises.

So this is how Patimile Mkhwebu finally married Lucy.

# An Unexpected Vacation

Once in the dreary years of our childhood my brother J and I scored ourselves a very nice vacation, which I've never forgotten. I can't remember exactly how young we were, but I know we were of an age when we should have been at primary school, yet J was working as a cattle herder for an old man called Pheleleni Maphosa in a nearby village and I was doing nothing – if you don't count roaming the bushes and picking berries every day from morning till sunset.

It happened some months after Baba and Mama split and Mama moved out and went to stay with Aunty Sbongile in Magwe. That was also shortly after Baba brought a girl called Meme to live with us, saying: 'Eeeeeee, this is your sister, Meme. Meme these are your brothers – Sipho and Joseph.'

Bango village was small at that time, the sun seemed to rise from the north, days and years felt long and slow. There were boys who were always fighting, knifing one another over two ugly sisters, while the village stood and watched. Then, when there was blood on the ground, someone would call a fat woman called MaNdiweni, who was always able to arbitrate.

We won this vacation in a very odd way – it came as a punishment. Mnyamana, the oldest goat in Baba's herd, gave birth in the forest and did not bring home the newborn. J and I did not notice until Baba found out on the evening of the second day.

'I want that kid found!' Baba shouted, his eyes ablaze with anger. He'd called us to his bedroom, and had us squatting on the dusty floor while he sat on the mattress of his bed. 'Who penned the goats today?'

'I did,' J said. When he was off work, J and I took turns penning the goats and doing all the household chores, though J resented this, feeling that because he was working and contributing food to the table, he'd outgrown children's chores.

'So you're telling me, Joseph, that at even your age you cannot tell when a pregnant goat has given birth?'

We were silent. J looked down, flushed and frightened.

Baba rose and shuffled out of his house. Soon he re-entered, and silently took off his boots, his hat and shirt, then sat on his bed for a while before quietly slipping into the sheets. It was his way of ignoring us and making us wonder whether or not he'd done with us or was merely considering what next to do or say. But seeing him in bed relieved us because we'd thought he'd whip us. When long minutes had elapsed, Baba said, 'We lose goats to jackals and disease. And now we lose them because of your negligence.' He sounded hurt. 'This cannot happen. Tomorrow I want to see Mnyamana with her kid. Close the door after you.' Then he pulled the blankets over his face and we scuttled out, relieved not to be beaten.

The next day we woke up at five, and entered the forest. We did not want him to wake up earlier than us and shoe us out of the house before we could dress, saying, 'Go! Go and find the kid! Go! Don't come back to my house until you've found it.'

Outside it was cold and dark though the sky in the east had begun to redden.

First we went to Bango Dam. It was scary because it was haunted by the spirits of two Grade 4 boys who'd been caught and drowned by a fishnet while swimming. But, still, that's where we went first and where we spent the morning picking berries in the surrounding bushes. By about ten we had each filled our two-kilogram plastic bags and our four pockets with bright red berries, so we sat beside a thicket on a white rock and feasted.

I think what actually won us that vacation was what we did afterwards. We never really searched for the kid, as we had set out to do. Rather, at midday, when we had finished the berries and were hungry again, we followed one another to Mkarabuli, where the crops were growing, and spent the afternoon stealing watermelons from Baba's field.

Now, when someone looks at it from the outside, they might say that we were not stealing because the field was the family's. But there's a difference, known perhaps, only to people who grew up in my village or in a village like it.

Although we were the ones who planted those watermelons with Baba, they were not really ours. To eat them, Baba would have to pick them, bring them home, slice them with his pocket knife, and divide them for us.

So what we were doing was theft and we knew it. And we knew we would be punished for it, and we were ready, only we never expected Baba would punish us the way he did. We'd expected the usual flogging to which we'd grown accustomed.

Baba had just returned from the search himself. We could see that when we arrived home in the evening, our stomachs big and round like women six months gone. He did not ask us whether we'd found the kid, but only where we'd looked. That was easy, we had memorised the story.

'First we went to Natshali's,' J said. J was not bright, but he was very good at lying. 'Then we went to SaMoffat's ruins and to the dam, passed at the hill, and crossed Gohole River, and into the field where they sometimes graze when they get mixed up with NaLukas's goats, but we couldn't find it.'

Baba looked at us strangely before disappearing into his house. We sat behind the kitchen near the fence like strangers because you failed to think what to do when you failed to do what Baba wanted. You could not play; you could not do anything that would make you happy. Doing anything felt like a crime; you simply had to wait in nervous anticipation until his anger burst out.

When Baba was angry, you felt the world thinning, suffocating you. You dreamt of places you'd never been to, of the kind of place you might never see in your life. We knew Baba was angry, but at

what, we did not know; we did not consider it possible that he coul.
have already heard about our day of feasting.

'NaZidiri says she saw you down north by the river? Why don't
you tell me about it?'

Baba's eyes were red. They were small eyes with thick eyelashes.
When he got angry, they fluttered like a heavy winged bird attempting to fly. He stared at J, occasionally dropping his angry glare on
me.

'I was mostly down by the hill. Why didn't I see you there? What
time did you pass through?'

The sun had turned westwards, but it still shone brightly, no longer hot but warm and good. A donkey-drawn cart passed down the
front street.

'Hhi? Speak Joseph! Why didn't I see you at the hill?'

Baba did not come to the kitchen for supper. He did not bath. He
did not go to pray with SaMadu, although it was Friday and he was
a pastor and supposed to be among the first to arrive at church. He
only came to fetch water in a jug to clean his teeth – something he
usually called Meme to do.

The following day we did not see him the whole morning, or the
whole afternoon. Once we thought that maybe he was sick. Especially when the sun turned westwards and he still hadn't appeared.
But then he showed up when the sun's rays, now cool and red, faded
behind the green mopani forest. Instead of coming out of his house,
as we had thought he would, he appeared through the gate, and
found us behind the back rondavel playing ntsoro, as we had done
the whole day.

He was with Babomncane Mpilo, Baba's only living sibling. He
lived at Homestead Village which was two villages away. You had to
pass Madala and Tswayini and walk a very long way down Gabuza
road to get there. Without a word, Baba and Babomncane Mpilo
passed us and proceeded to Baba's house where they locked themselves in.

J and I didn't say anything to one another. But we both knew
things were not good; Baba had found out and he was mad; but why
he had gone to fetch Babomncane Mpilo we had no idea.

For a long time Babomncane Mpilo and Baba talked behind the locked door. That day, supper was late – we usually had it at eight but Meme only cooked at nine because she'd gone to fetch firewood with her friends and returned home late.

It was around ten when Babomncane Mpilo came to tell us that Baba wanted to see us. It was very late for us. We were preparing to sleep. We slept in the kitchen, J, me and Meme.

The first thing we saw when we entered Baba's house was a bulky white sack at the side of the door, and an empty shell of a watermelon on the floor. Next to Baba, on a four-person wooden bench, sat Ncube, the headman, and three pastors from our church: pastors Dube, Ngulube and Sbeko. When they'd arrived, I never knew. J and I squatted on the dusty floor, near the door. Baba was speaking, but I couldn't make out what he was saying; I was busy thinking, with insurmountable fright, of what was going to happen to us. We had known stealing watermelons was suicidal, but we hadn't anticipated that so many people would be involved.

'I'm tired Ncube,' Baba was saying when his words finally entered my ears. 'I really am.'

Everyone was silent. And Baba continued.

'They ask for more food at supper. You beat them for it, they don't give up. This Joseph here,' – he pointed at J as if some did not know him – 'works at Tswayini. He would bring the milk and then drink it again like a cat. They can't even look after the goats. You tell them this is wrong, they do it. You beat them for it, they don't stop. What am I to do? Kill myself? Kill them? No, Ncube! I can't live with such children. Heaven be praised I exercised enough self-restraint not to kill them on the spot. I'm through with these children.'

'At the end of the day, they're your kids, Moyo,' Pastor Sbeko said.

'I've never had such children as these. I raised Bigboy, I raised Ntando, I raised Abraham, and they are all good, respectable people. I have a good track record as a father.'

'And I refuse to be molested in old age,' Baba added as an afterthought.

He was silent for a little while and so was everyone. He stood up and then he sat down, muttering. Long minutes passed. And then

Pastor Dube interposed, 'You can't do that, Moyo. They're only kids.'
'No, they're demons incarnate!' Baba snapped.

There was another even tenser silence. 'Moyo, you can't do this!'
Pastor Sbeko spoke.

'Somebody try to stop me. I'll kill them and kill myself.'

You could tell that he meant it. He was losing it. They all tried to
talk him down but Baba was too angry. He said that anyone who
wanted to take us and make us their own children was free to do so,
but he wanted nothing to do with us again for as long as he lived. He
paced up and down, whispering, and occasionally telling the men
the meeting was over.

When all attempts to make Baba change his mind had failed,
Babomncane Mpilo took us with him. We stayed at Homestead
Village for three months and had an unforgettable time. Mostly because many things that Baba disallowed, were allowed at Babomncane's. My cousins went to swim in the river on hot days, they asked
for more food when they were not full, and they even threw away
surplus sadza. This act was eye-opening for me. I'd never imagined
that there were people with enough food to throw away.

At the beginning of the autumn, we returned home. Babomncane
Mpilo took us back. He said Baba was missing us badly.

Indeed Baba was happy to see us. He even hugged us which he
had never done before. Smiling, he asked us where we'd been, and
said he had searched for us everywhere – at Bango Dam, on the
other side of Gohole River; he'd begun to worry that we'd been kid-
napped by ngungas, supposed child thieves of those days. He even
told us that Nontobana and Mpunga had given birth to two plump
dappled kids which we would instantly love.

In the evening we slaughtered a goat. Baba supervised as Musa
cooked. Babomncane Mpilo's wife and children arrived at sunset to
spend the night. That only happened at Christmas but Baba said a wel-
come ceremony was necessary; and so we sang and danced and told
folktales with our cousins in the moonlight as if it were Christmas.

Baba and Babomncane Mpilo sat with a paraffin lamp on their
table and talked a lot: arguing, raising their voices, and laughing.

'Things have changed,' Bobomncane said with food in his mouth, ne hand reaching into the bowl of sadza.

'Indeed,' answered Baba.

'Children can now ask for more sadza at supper, as if that were normal. I remember when we grew up, that was unthinkable.'

'A taboo,' Baba added, laughing.

And as we sat having our own meal, J and I wondered if we could disobey Baba again and enjoy another vacation, but somehow it seemed as if the rules had changed.

# Apathy

## 51/49

It was on the 17th November in a year I shall not mention, in a country I'd rather not mention, that an old man who'd held the highest office for too many decades, seeking to appear principled and steadfast, uttered a lie pernicious to the wellbeing of the citizens. He thought his countrymen stupid. They were not, of course, and they knew that what the old man had told them was a self-seeking untruth and they were aware of how badly it would affect their lives, but they ignored it. So total was this attitude that you'd think people had conspired to achieve it.

The following morning on a road to a primary school in a village in the south, children in fading khaki uniforms did not talk about the old man or allude to his untruth, instead, as always, they argued about wrestling, their fathers, holidays on the ranches, books, tests, exams, homework and unfair teachers. Some nonchalantly kicked about a plastic football scoring indifferent goals on the roadside. They saw no reason to change just because the old man had said what he'd said.

And so it was at the primary school, with teachers saying good morning to one another, some gossiping, others asking for paraffin or making small talk to pass the time. Some stood in the sun, waiting for assembly, complaining about lazy children and exercises still waiting to be marked. And when the bell rang, and the students arrived and gathered at assembly, so did all the teachers.

It was then that a short teacher called MaNkala, the wife of Headmaster Ncube, without saying a word about the old man or showing any strain or sign of anger, detached herself from other teachers. Then when all the children were quiet and attentive, she climbed the small flagstone podium, stood next to the flagpost and said 'Good morning Children' in a loving voice. After they had reciprocated, she asked for a 'chorus please' and a boy called Bhunku with a thin but not unsatisfactory voice began 'There is no one like you my Jehovah'. And as he sang, the teacher kept a straight face, not thinking about what the old man had said, but only about her present duty. So that when the boy had finished, she asked that they sing the national anthem. A clean girl, probably the cleanest in school, raised the national flag standing on the podium next to MaNkala. And when that was over, her face calm and untroubled, MaNkala went on to read verses from the Bible, verses about respect for elderly people, the power of God, and the ten commandments. She gave no sign, none whatever, to indicate that she knew what the old man had said the day before and how pernicious a lie it was. MaNkala did things calmly and by the book, as if everything was fine, as if she were stupid.

Afterwards, beginning with the first grades, the students marched to their respective classrooms, accompanied by the song 'Moses saw a burning tree' begun by Bhunku, who sang as if he didn't know what the old man had said.

A tall teacher with glasses, who was also the sports' master, a man who loved to laugh, and was very handsome and good at football, came to his Grade 6 class carrying a book, a metre rule and two pieces of chalk.

'Where were we yesterday, guys?' he asked in his normal voice, his face showing no strain, his eyes clear as running water, and when a bright boy called Melusi, his voice clear and normal, told him that they were doing long division, the teacher said, 'Turn to page 162,' and waited, face blank, as the *prrrr prrrr* of page-turning took place. And when everyone was ready, his voice clear, he explained a few concepts, wrote a little on the blackboard, made a few jokes, and ordered his pupils to write Exercise 4a and submit their work later that day. If you didn't know the tall teacher and didn't know what the old man had said, you'd think everything was all right; you'd think the teacher knew of no pernicious lies spoken by an old man on the previous day. But the teacher had heard the lie, and as someone capable of thinking, he knew what the words meant and that things would never be the same again. Yet he did not say anything, he did not even think about it. Nothing. Not even a grumble such as 'my old mother is pension-less and you keep talking about…!' No. He did not say anything like that at all.

Apathy was everywhere. In the towns, in the villages, in the buses and the bars, in the fields and in the factories: everywhere.

The young bearded mechanic, in a town I will not mention, told the truck driver whose vehicle he'd just fixed, 'You didn't check the oil. If you had, your truck wouldn't have burnt its bearings.'

Even the fence-mender whom the children of a particular primary school in a particular village passed as he trailed three large mopani logs to his field, knew what the old man had said. But he continued to call out, 'Wo-ho-ho…' to his donkeys, raising his whip now and then, and turning to the young man beside him to confirm, that now we've mended the eastern side we should focus on the northern fence. And then we can rest.

Similarly in three miserable huts in a sad village, the name of which I shall not mention, a woman older than her age sat on a floursack mat under a lemon tree together with her husband, talking about food: wondering where they would find it, and concerned for their children whom they did not wish to starve. Neither said anything about what the old man had said, even though they knew well how pernicious such talk was, and that because of it, their lives would never be the same again; and if ever they wanted better lives, they would have to go to another country where old men who held such big offices did not utter such pernicious lies, and if they ever did, were held accountable.

Everyone, countrywide, knew the old man's past, the things he'd said and done and that everything was punctuated by his history.

ne people ignored him, hoping that one day he would stop talking and die because he was an old man. Some of them wondered if he really thought they believed him when with his usual rhetoric, he pointed at ghosts and demons of the past, and the West, as the cause of their poverty and suffering, while in fact his greed was to blame for the harshness in their lives. Yet instead of speaking, people only shook their heads, sneered a little, saying *'Nc! Nc! Lomuntu!* This person! He thinks we're foolish.'

You would think they were quiet because they were afraid. And, yes, it was risky talking about the old man, or even referring to him. You had to be careful about what you said. But the apathy wasn't about that. People simply preferred to focus on their day-to-day activities. Who would want to have this order disturbed? People simply wanted to go weeding in their fields every morning, return home for tea at eleven, and talk about their crops and their goats.

My grandmother is dying of starvation in the rural areas! A middle-aged man, light skinned, wearing a vest, told the men who played at the pool table with him in a nondescript tavern on the outskirts of a city I'd also rather not mention. His friend said that if elderly people received old-age pensions, as they did in other countries, life would be easier. Instead they exchanged stories of dependence:

'My family depends on my brother in Windhoek.'

'Our aunt in London sent us money for Christmas.'

'My father works in Johannesburg.'

If they drew closer in, it was only to say, 'He thinks we don't know. He thinks we're stupid.' They never said anything more than that.

Everyone had seen the old man lie and knew what it meant for them and their children and the children of their children, but they said nothing. The televisions continued playing, and the few working men returned to their families in the evening and talked about what had happened at their workplace, the taste of food, their uniforms having to be washed and ironed, the hot weather and of what they'd seen or heard during the day. Nobody said, 'No, I'm not going to work tomorrow because of what the old man has said.'

The old man, who had stood upright on a podium, wearing a

green suit and blinking abnormally, had offered many harmle.
untruths prior to saying this most pernicious of lies. And when he
spoke, it had been received with a rapturous applause by members
of his delegation. Not that they believed him. They knew too that he
was lying but it was their job to applaud him. However, so vile was
the lie and its implications for the livelihood of the ordinary elders
of the country, children going to school, mothers and fathers, young
men and women getting married, everyone in the country except
the old man and his family and friends, that, if nature intervened,
or reacted to the lie, nothing short of an earthquake would have
occurred.

The apathy was not only in people. It spread across the hills,
across rivers, across mountains, across large dams; it penetrated the
crevices in the rocks and echoed in long uninhabited stretches of
land, confirmed by stalwart donkeys here and there which braved
the sun to graze. The apathy was manifest in the normalcy of life,
in the trees continuing to grow, in the sky continuing to be free of
clouds, in the ground continuing to be hot at noon because of the
sun, nature being unmoved. No natural pattern of life was disturbed
despite that what the old man had said had so pernicious an effect
on the people, that it would not have been surprising had the sky
and the ground come together in protest. The man who killed his
wife after she busted him in bed with another woman hadn't done as
much wrong as the old man. Yet for the former, a swift reaction took
place as he was soon arrested and locked up in prison.

The apathy prevailed in the large trees, in the bushes, in hospi-
tals, at libraries, at police stations; it prevailed at registrar offices,
at meetings among villagers across the country; it prevailed everywhere. The only place you could not find it was at meetings of the
executives of big companies operating in the country. The fifty-one
or forty-nine per cent lay central to their concerns and their profits.

# Death by Cell Phone

Had it not been that his son, who was living overseas, promised to call him at 2 p.m., Mdala Moyo would have left his cell phone at home, and that way, the villagers would never have killed him.

But the Friday of the ceremony coincided with the aforementioned call; to ignore it would have been letting hunger eat his family as they depended upon his son's remittances; yet to absent himself from the ceremony would also have been suicidal.

So what did Mdala Moyo do? He took his cell phone to the ceremony with him stashed in the little pouch under the right armpit of his sleeveless ox-hide jacket, hoping that towards 2.00 p.m., he'd slip into a nearby bush as if to relieve his bowels, and then quietly receive his call.

Mdala Moyo was among the earliest to arrive at the king's homestead, where the ceremony was held. He enjoyed a laugh with the two elderly men at the gate and was in a particularly good mood. Wearing his beautiful hide clothes which he'd bartered for a bucket of millet from Buzi, the village merchant who had a shop near the deserted primary school, Mdala appeared youthful. His early arrival also granted him the pleasure of witnessing the king lambast Milos, a former cellist from Gudu village, for his reluctance to hold a ceremony and reclaim his rightful surname lost a century ago, when his great-grandfather was adopted by the Lungus. Mdala Moyo stored the incident as an anecdote to tell his wife. She'd not been able to come because of a headache that had tormented her for nearly a week.

When the sun was high and a man called Ghandi called people to assemble inside the Great Tower that had been built by the villagers to resemble the symbol of one of Africa's proudest ancient civilisations, Mdala Moyo was among the first to enter, and behold, not out of interest but duty, the many artefacts or implements, displayed within the vast interior.

The Barosi People's Cultural Practice Ceremony had been established by the king, a few years after the country returned to black majority rule. He'd lambasted the revolutionary regime in Gokwe as a 'Western puppet', pointing out that it was doing nothing to restore the values which, after all, had been fought for; but instead perpetuating the colonial agenda in the name of economic development. The purpose of the ceremony, he'd stated, was to right that wrong, giving the African man his pride by restoring lost values.

The villagers sat on the polished mud floor, men to the east, women to the west, facing each other, in accordance with the pre-colonial traditions of the Barosi people.

The business of the ceremony began with the king thanking the villagers for what he termed the greatest achievement they had so far made, which was banning Western education in the Kingdom.

'For, comrades,' the king said, 'we cannot realistically tell ourselves that we're truly free when our children go to Western schools to be told that the black man was subjugated by the white man because he was weak, and the white man sought to civilise him. That's madness.'

The villagers cheered loudly.

Fist clenched and energetically pumping it into the air, the king sought the villagers' confirmation that they were ready to defend, tooth and bone, all the values that had been restored in their area so far to absolute, irreversible decolonisation.

The villagers, fists in the air, shouted in cacophonous affirmation.

'We cannot trust the Gokwe regime,' the king said. 'A bunch of hypocrites who would murder us in our sleep to have their ways. We should unite comrades, and always be watchful.'

Again the people whooped and cheered.

'Our road has not been easy,' the king continued. 'When we began, no one could have imagined that one day all of us would be proudly living in mud huts like our ancestors, living without vile Western phones, ignoring all these unsightly water taps the imperialists' friends have installed in our village. Who could have imagined we could all be of the same mind? Dressing like our ancestors? Using no Western gadgets and happy in our own ways? This is magical, comrades. Our victory from colonialism will inspire many village folk in this country to follow our example. They will learn that you do not need corrupt Western money to buy goods in our village; they will learn that our children are taught not corrupt words and ideas, but manual labour necessary to sustain a life.'

Mdala Moyo felt a boundless love for the king. 'Your wisdom and prudence will outlive you, honourable one,' he formed the words in his mouth but fell short of spitting them out.

As every year, the main speech at the ceremony was delivered by Thembani, the king's son, whom it was rumoured had received the best Western education, though before the king had realised his contempt for the West.

He was preceded by a band of traditional dancers, which consisted of six girls and six boys. Singing a song about a black goat used as oblation to the ancestors, they abraded the floor with their feet. Not to be left out, Mdala Moyo joined them, swaying his big stomach and half-clothed haunches.

Then Thembani rose from where he sat among young men and strode to the front. Like most young men, he carried a spear and a shield, which he placed near his feet.

'Last year?' he said, moving about, rubbing his hands together.

'We removed our children from Western schools after discovering that they did not exist during the times of our ancestors.' The villagers shouted uproariously.

'Last of last year?'

We killed and burned all the skinless yellow people in our village, in accordance with our ancestors' tradition of cleaning communities.'

'Last of last of last year?'

'We promoted our chief into king, and made our ward a kingdom, after discovering that before colonialism our ancestors weren't ruled by chiefs but by kings and lived not in wards but kingdoms.'

'This year?'

'We give our chief a regiment, reclaim the Mbuzi village goldfields and expel the foreigners so we can mine them ourselves, just like our ancestors once did.'

'Next year?'

'We will use force to expel Gokwe from all the territory under the Barosi Kingdom.'

This was Thembani's much loved rhetoric. It boosted his confidence as much as it incited the villagers to follow his lead.

Continuing with startling vigour, he shouted out the names of several Barosi historical figures whom he hailed as fathers of various modern scientific fields, and the people whooped and cheered, for those names ignited the fire of nationalist passions in everyone's heart. This was to remind the villagers of the motto: Pre-colonial Africa possessed everything the West had, only in different forms.

'Comrades,' Thembani declaimed in his high-pitched voice, as he moved about. 'It is with great honour that I find myself, as in years past, standing before you, tasked with this lofty responsibility.'

Mdala Moyo sat slumped forward, his head in his hands, not missing a word. Thembani's speech always aroused an unquenchable patriotic passion. He could well imagine, in fact he almost thought he'd experienced, the perfect ancient past, long before white people knew of the existence of Africa.

'Although considering my age,' Thembani continued, 'I'm the least qualified to be speaking about so grave a subject; but my purpose in standing before you is not to recount the dastardly deeds of white people upon our ancestors but that of identifying what traditions, what culture, what identity can still be recovered from the pollution the white man left behind.'

'Ehe-e-e! Ehe-e-e!' Mdala Moyo was among the many elderly men who gravely affirmed these words.

'We're a wounded people, comrades,' Thembani rasped. 'Colonialism wounded us, and dressing those wounds would not have been so hard had it not been for the fact that the same dogs that bit us in the past are still lurking in the shadows, baying for more of our blood by peddling democracy and diplomacy.'

The villagers whooped and grunted and some threw their hands in the air.

'Down with Gokwe!' they shouted with one voice.

'I tell you what comrades. We're not a free people. Colonialism never ended. Why, our natural resources are still whisked away every day in broad daylight to develop the same countries that only yesterday denied us our liberties.'

A man stood up and sang a liberation war song, gambolling about and waving his hands. Many people joined him, until Thembani raised his arms and voice over the din.

'So I say to you my fellow villagers,' he continued, 'let's continue to despise everything that smells of the West. Because, you might not realise that it could be a cell phone, a TV or a car or a wheelbarrow; it could just be a pair of sunglasses, some hair extensions, or some perfumed soap, items that can lull you into indifference, their colonial trap. We must never let our guard drop. Our ancestors made do with none of these items, why can't we?'

'Why can't we?' echoed the men at Thembani's feet, Mdala Moyo among them.

'The first step,' Thembani continued, 'would be to educate the youth in our own version of history. The fact that before Europeans came to Africa we mined gold and iron and traded in silver and jewellery, we imported and exported, we processed our own diamonds and made machines, which we sold to India and many other Asian countries. We should educate our youth about great men like Chandita Inui, Chigubu Chiyangwa, Ziwoto Zenusi, they must know of the great cities these people built, of the cosmic discoveries they made, our children should know that science started right here in Africa!'

Pride so intense it felt like anguish filled everyone's heart. The villagers, in one mass, rose and threw their clenched fists into the air, shouting 'AFRICA! AFRICA!' These names filled the villagers' hearts with so much strength and euphoria that some felt that Africa was a land of everything – miracles, science and magic. As for Mdala Moyo he felt so happy and so powerful he fancied he could move the world.

'I'm not going to lie and say that before the Europeans came to Africa we had no wars, no droughts, and no diseases,' Thembani continued, awakening those whose imagination was transported back into the past. 'No comrades! Those things existed as they do in all nations. But I wouldn't be lying when I say the white man brought more wars, more suffering and more diseases – some of which are incurable – and, above all, he robbed the black man of his source of livelihood, like the woodman chopping down the trunk of a tree and replacing it with an artificial one.'

There was a sudden click of the tongues in reaction to the simile, one which Thembani drew upon every year as it never failed to arouse deep loathing for the white people among the villagers.

'Down with Europeans!' a section of the crowd shouted.

'There are some among us,' continued Thembani, 'who have, to the detriment of our unity, sadly opted to remain linked to the European colonisers. These people are like children who can be fooled with sweets. Like the puppet government in Gokwe, they believe they cannot do without mobile phones, without cars, without big Western styled houses, without Western clothes. I say they have no place here.'

'They have no place in the Barosi Kingdom,' cried the villagers in unison.

This is what reminded Mdala Moyo of his dilemma. But because he had no watch, he could never have imagined how close to 2 p.m. it was, so he allowed himself to think that it was still early. Then a man called Bhedla beside him started a song, and it lulled Mdala Moyo into complete forgetfulness and the old man promised himself that after the ceremony he would seek out this Bhedla fellow and ask him where he found the lyrics. The song, which the villagers rose to their feet as they sang it, ran:

'Foxy white people
You stole our resources
*You stole our dignity*

71

*And disrupted our ways!*
*You stole our livelihood*
*You stole our happiness*
*But beware now foxy-fox*
*Because we're reclaiming everything!*
*And never again*
*Never never never again*
*Shall our people suffer*
*Suffer from your possessions!'*

The villagers sang along euphorically.

After this Thembani drew his speech to a conclusion through the motto of the Barosi people: 'Pre-colonial Africa possessed everything the West had though in different forms'.

It probably was the adrenalin caused by this rhetoric that caused Mdala Moyo to forget everything, even the phone in his pocket. In any case, he was an old man, not bright enough to remember two things at once. So, when minutes later, his cell phone rang with the ringtone of a song 'Emotional Rescue' by the American rock band 'Rolling Stones', a song his grandson based in the city had set for him when he was home on holiday, Mdala Moyo was as alarmed as everyone around him, as to who could be bold as to desecrate so pure a ceremony.

For a long while complete stupefied silence fell on the gathering. Then someone cried, 'Traitor!' and the villagers threw themselves at Mdala Moyo, who sprang to his feet and took to his heels. When he reached the courtyard, a spear grazed his thigh while two clubs whooshed past his skull, with the force of a cyclone.

Mdala Moyo forgot where the gate was and climbed the wooden fence that marked the perimeter of the king's homestead. Here he was almost caught by the leg, but he managed to jump free. When he landed on the other side, he was already panting like a dying cow, but he continued running.

'Stop right there you two-timer!' cried a hoarse voice from among his pursuers.

'Gokwe friend!' cried another voice.

They chased him through the sparse acacia scrub that was immediately in front of the king's homestead, and into the mopane forest and past the deserted Mbewu fields.

Glancing back and panting heavily, he noticed that the two dozen elderly men who were chasing him were the king's policemen, most of whom were his drinking friends, though now as they pursued him, they had assumed grim strangers' visages. Thankfully there weren't any young men among them who could have easily caught him. This was in accordance with the Barosi's people's rules of dealing with traitors, which forbade the involvement of young people.

As the distance increased, some men lagged, and at the end there were fewer than ten men in hot pursuit.

Mdala Moyo prudently called out from afar, that his wife and grandchildren should lock themselves in the kitchen. She heard him but ignored his call, and stood watching, transfixed. But when she saw him appear, his heels almost hitting his occiput, she obeyed and scurried into the kitchen with the grandchildren. Only a beast could be after him, she speculated before she realised it a band of his elderly friends in hot and angry pursuit.

Mdala Moyo lived with his wife and three grandchildren. All his children were away, some married, some working in the city, one overseas. His wife opened the door for him, then locked the door with an iron smith's wedge. They hoped they were safe but they were not.

In leaps and bounds, and barking like hounds after a hare, the men approached. 'Makadliwe!' screamed the voice of a man Mdala Moyo thought belonged to Dliwayo, one of his many friends.

'If I get out of this alive I will teach myself to choose my friends more carefully,' Mdala Moyo told himself, as he collapsed onto a stool. His sweat streamed onto the shiny floor. The grandchildren had huddled frightened in the corner. Mdala Moyo's wife was still repeating the question she had greeted him with, 'What's happening?' But he hadn't the mind to answer.

'Comrades,' I can explain,' Mdala Moyo said as a loud bang came from the door.

'Traitor!' shouted a voice that Mdala Moyo identified as that of Ncube, a mate from the MaNdlovu beerhall, whom on many occasions had borrowed his axe.

'Open the door or we'll knock it down. Traitor!'

'Let's set the hut alight,' someone suggested.

'No,' another objected, 'we should get him alive so that other traitors will learn from him what is done to their kind.

'Comrades,' cried Mdala Moyo, 'I'm not a traitor. I can explain. See, as some of you know, I've a son overseas, we communicate through...'

'Traitor ...!' the same voice repeated.

BANG! BANG! The door was attacked and when it finally gave, three or four men bounded in, while others stood at the door.

'The traitor must be killed,' the men cried.

'Comrades, comrades, please!' cried Mdala Moyo. Yet they approached him, clubs upraised, none flinching from sympathy. One club landed on the kneeling Mdala Moyo's head and set him sprawling unconscious. The second and the third, both delivered by Masotsha, a tanner from Mbuzi village, ended Mdala Moyo's life.

'What is done about the traitor's wife and grandchildren?' asked Buthelezi, who was among the men who were holding Mdala Moyo's weeping wife, and guarding the terrified children from escape.

'He'll be taken to the king,' said Ngulube, a jovial elderly man who was regarded as the best potter in all the villages under the kingdom. 'The king will decide their fate.'

Some shrieked in horror upon seeing Mdala Moyo's modern mugs, pots and plates, stacked alongside the earthen ones. It was clear from the way they were placed in the mud cupboard that the earthen utensils weren't used, but were merely ornamental relics. An aluminium pot, from which a maize meal had been cooked, lay unwashed.

'We've been living with a fox, badala,' said Dliwayo.

Meanwhile others folded the dead Mdala Moyo into a blanket as was done in the past, to be presented to the king. And while this was happening, others were setting alight Mdala Moyo's homestead, burning down the three huts, which they had, after searching, found that it contained many vile western things.

They stood watching dispassionately as flames shot to the skies and the smoke billowed in clouds.

And when all was done, the men sat under the mopani tree that stood near the gate of Mdala Moyo's homestead. And slowly, as the feeling of betrayal that had possessed them and provoked them to action, subsided, gloominess fell upon them. Remembering their dead friend, forced them to consider the harshness of their action. They had drunk beer with him, joked with him, co-operated with him on many things, but in one moment of lust for blood, they had taken his life and it was painful to each of them. Yet they did not speak their feelings and each dealt with it in his own way.

Looking into the mopani tree, Ngulube saw a traditional water-cooler hanging from a branch, and brought it down. All men were thirsty after so exhausting a task, and they took turns drinking the cool water from it. It was tap water, everyone realised this but neither spoke of it nor stopped drinking. The river was seven kilometres from his home, the tap just two.

Returning to the king's homestead later, they did not speak about Mdala Moyo again, but he was still in their minds, his absence pervading the very air they breathed.

They arrived to find the king talking about plans to establish a regiment, so the gold fields in Mbuzi village could be repossessed from foreigners and fund a war that he planned to wage against the imperialist-serving regime in Gokwe.

'Are you with me, comrades?'

'Yes,' shouted the villagers.

'Gokwe must fall!'

'Down and crumble into smithereens!'

The ceremony would have ended on a jubilant note but for the news the king's policemen brought on their arrival that Mdala Moyo, one of the most enthusiastic of their number, and a friend to all, was not only a traitor but dead. Each man too wondered deep in his heart if he did not have some Western gadget on which he depended and would be loathe to part with.

# The Face of Reality

At twenty-nine years of age Ezekiel Nkomo was still cramped with his parents in a three-roomed RDP house. That's because he considered himself a writer and wanted his career to take off before he faced life by himself. The RDP was a sombre little house built for poor South Africans by their government; his family rented it because they were illegal immigrants from Zimbabwe and weren't qualified for social grants. He had neither friends nor girlfriends. He lived within the solitude provided by the bare walls of his tiny bedroom, reassured by the illusory fantasies which promised him a future so bright even a president's daughter might wish to share with him.

Ezekiel was a tall, thin young man with skin the colour of coal. Coal was also the nickname the boys had called him during high school. He had a large face from which a large forehead disconcertingly protruded. He was writing a movie script about the affluent life of a beggar who stumbled upon fifty million rands in a Jo'burg dustbin. Notwithstanding a dozen other such scripts he'd unsuccessfully written, he sincerely believed that this one would prove his ticket to millionairedom.

When he was not writing, Ezekiel offered carpet-cleaning services and used the little money he earned to buy books, clothes and promote his scripts in the American screenwriting contests. Every day, after washing the dishes, he went to the library, returning home in the evening. Every day in the middle of his writing, he paused to contemplate his loveless life. Sometimes he was overwhelmed by the thought that life was passing him by. But mostly he chose to be philosophical. The prospect of failure, of aging sad and alone, like his biological father back in the village, frightened him.

Thus he had lived for many years, his life rolling on smoothly – an adventureless tale – until two girls came along and gave his orderly life a shake.

The first one was Elizabeth. He met her in the library. He was returning his laptop to its bag, preparing to leave, when he heard a small voice from behind him, say, 'I have a laptop and a modem at home but I can't connect to the internet. What do you think is the problem?'

He turned around at once and saw a plain girl. She did not compare with the women of his fantasies. Her thick lips, short skirt, and brown hair, which appeared as if fried in hair oil, did not give him the impression of a girl seeking to be noticed by men; but he was to remember that simple face for a very long time because standing there looking at her, it struck him that he'd just met the best woman he could find, plain and simple, the one he'd always needed without knowing it.

'You have a modem,' he repeated, '... and yet you can't connect to the internet... do you know how to do it? I mean, have you checked the drivers?' He put his bag onto his shoulders and started out beside her.

They walked together out of the library into the grey street, past the Community Skills Centre until they stopped to chat near the brown hills where their ways diverged. She told him she was a student nurse at a nearby clinic working towards a degree. He told her he was an aspiring screenwriter with several dozen rejected screenplays under his belt. She was impressed and said he certainly was the most tenacious person she had ever met.

Writing, he told her, was not a career choice, he had not had the opportunity to 'choose' a career perhaps in sports or academics.

'Same with me,' she said, smiling and saying that she chose nursing because it was the only available opportunity open to her.

He liked her passion and told her it matched his and she was pleased. She said she found it hard to balance her schoolwork and her job and with every year that passed before she qualified as a professional, her frustration increased. He said he felt exactly the same way. And they were both pleased to have unexpectedly found one another and they talked among other things about the lazy youth of today; how fast the years rolled by; and how hard it was to make something of oneself. She had considerable knowledge of world affairs and he was glad to have met her.

By the time they parted – she going past Great Hem Mall to where she lived at Ext. 3B, and he going past the garage towards Evaton – he already knew that she lived with her working mother and a good-for-nothing brother who was only seen at home at dinner in the evenings. He felt that he could kill for her. But she denied him her phone number.

'No, I don't give my number to strangers,' she said.

'But I feel like I've known you my whole life,' he protested.

'I'm sorry but we've just met,' she was adamant.

In the following days he went to the library only to look for her. At first he thought she only meant to test his commitment, so he did not lose hope but kept up his pursuit. But when after months she remained aloof, his heart began to sink.

'If I'm going to give in to a man,' she told him as they walked past the mall one day. 'I need to know he really loves me. What happened to the tradition of a man having to pursue a woman for years? Because a boy thinks he can woo a girl in just a day is the reason why so many couples break-up nowadays.'

This renewed his resolve. Sometimes he would feel her close to giving in; she would promise him her phone numbers and tell him about her insecurities; that she needed a man who would not let her down, a man ready to commit, yet the next day she would be of a different mind, and she would tell him she did not need a man in her life. She was just fine. She had learned to live without men, and she was happy.

For all the four or so months he paid her court, though inconsistently because of her infrequent visits to the library, he never found out why she continuously shut him out when she seemed to be so at ease around him. She'd made it clear she did not want anybody visiting her at home: so when she stopped coming to the library, that was the end of that. But as the months passed, he felt as if he'd been cheated of a chance of happiness.

Nonetheless the encounter provoked in him an unquenchable urge to find love. He gave his writing secondary attention as he embarked on a mission to find a woman who would walk the last mile with him, as he imagined the years before his big breakthrough occurred. But all his efforts were fruitless. Most girls turned him down while others merely teased him; and those who were interested were not to his taste.

After a year of fruitless endeavour, he forced himself to forget about girls and return to his writing. But one day, while he lay on his bed, he remembered a girl called Amanda whom he'd met way back. He checked her on Facebook, found her cell phone number, and called her. She agreed to meet him.

He'd known her back in the village and they'd once met in Jo'burg but apart from the coincidence of two villagers meeting in a big city, she'd shown him indifference.

They met near her place and sat on the veranda of a grocery store and reminisced about their high school days. She told him she'd been scared of boys then, which is why she ran away when boys wanted to court her.

She was not exactly beautiful. He knew better looking women. Her teeth were gapped and her unpainted lips were the colour of canned beef. Her legs were too thin and rickety and her short hair dyed brown made her look like a boy. She was also too short. A brown, burn scar at the back of her hand repulsed him. Her tightly fitting black dress that completely covered her breasts was also unattractive. Not to mention her restiveness; she could not sit still for a minute.

But he was surprised at how vulnerable he felt because despite all his misgivings, deep down he knew she was simply the right girl for him. His mother would approve of her, everyone would, even his uncle who lived in Thathe. They would approve even more when he told them that he'd known her since childhood and she was now studying at university. So he forced himself to love her and everything about her.

He bought a Fanta which they drank slowly, chatting. They talked about the political situation at home and reminisced about high school days; she brought out her tablet and showed him pictures of her family, brothers and sisters, her mother and grandfather, pictures of her celebrating her 21st birthday in the village, pictures taken during her holidays. Ezekiel interpreted this display as love.

She never said she loved him, he simply assumed it; no woman would declare their love – actions spoke louder than words.

Over the following days they chatted on Facebook and at night he said good night, dream about us, and she replied, 'you too'. He composed a quiz and and she responded asking him to choose between love colours. His answer was vague, but when he asked her to choose, she chose orange, which to those who played this game signified 'love'. At this his heart leapt up, and he tried to manoeuvre her into saying she loved him, and when she wouldn't, he did not press her.

Over the following days he could not write because his mind was preoccupied with Amanda. He kept imagining himself with her; walking in a park, living in a beautiful, spacious house in a suburb; saving her from some huge calamity to become her eternal hero.

They arranged to meet on a Tuesday, and she had promised she would come with him to see where he lived. So, on Monday he spent the day cleaning his tiny bedroom. He fixed the electricity cables that for years had hung intertwined at the head of his bed, and shifted the bed to sweep the dirt that had accumulated underneath it.

Then he called her but she apologised and said she was at varsity. On the next day she said she had a toothache and was going to clinic. But on the third day she agreed to meet him.

They met at the same spot, sat on the veranda of the shop, with her brother's plump girlfriend buzzing about. He was still in the same shirt and trousers in which he had been dressed during their first encounter because many people had told him they fitted him nicely. She was in different attire; a short, tight-fitting skirt, wedge hcels and a short loose top that left her stomach bare. He felt weak upon seeing her and he did not know whether to pour his heart out. But before he could decide, before there was any conversation, one thing led to another and another and the end result was that she declared: 'And what then… because I don't love you,'

It was an honest statement. He felt weak, and wanted to stand up right then and say good bye, or to ask her straight out if she'd been patronising him.

But he restrained himself and made small talk until she went into the shop, chatted with her brother's girlfriend, and shortly afterwards reappeared with a litre of Fanta and two glasses, smiling her words, 'My skwiza has bought us a drink.'

They sipped their drinks and an old lady, a relative of hers appeared with whom Amanda talked until she was ready to leave. He did not ask her to stay longer but instead gave her a brief lecture about the benefits of finding someone who 'loves you  more than you love them,' and pointing out that there is usually a gap between 'what you want and what is good for you.' She only laughed and when he asked her what was so funny, she only laughed the more.

He felt the urge to cry as he walked home down a dusty path. Never before had he been so hopeful about a girl. But Amanda had killed his hope with a single statement: 'What then…because I don't love you.' He knew that Amanda didn't have a boyfriend, but clearly would not want to have one like him. For the first time he understood something he'd always been too pre-occupied to grasp. So when he entered his bedroom, he took the half mirror that lay on top of his well-made bed, and looked at himself. He felt sorry for the man he saw reflected. How different from the man within.  He felt a cold shiver come over him and he realised it was fear, fear of life.

He took off his T-shirt and lay supine letting his mind wander over many things, while staring at the nail holes in the roof. He wondered if he would ever achieve his goals or if his efforts were merely farce and escapism. A loss of passion for all the splendour of the world, for all the things he had 'put off until he could afford them', suddenly came over him and he felt more afraid.

After some time, he got up, put on his T-shirt, and went outside.

For a long time he stood under the peach tree in the yard and gazed at the yellow bond houses on the other side of the street: beautiful houses. He felt that love did not suit him and doubted that he would ever find it. A girl he'd loved once, tired of his persistence, had likened him to a gorilla. He had chosen to believe she was only trying to put him down but now he suspected that a semblance of truth was immanent in her undiplomatic comparison. Ugliness was his malady, something you could never defeat. Poverty you could work hard and overcome; xenophobia could by evaded by a return to your own country; illness could be treated. But his malady was one from which there was neither respite nor remedy. And sadness overcame him.

In the following days he had neither appetite for food nor the inspiration to write. Even his mother noticed that something was bothering him, but when she asked, he only groaned and told her that his latest screenplay had been rejected.

The end of the torment occurred one insomniac night when he lay musing and it suddenly occurred to him that before he met Elizabeth and Amanda, his life had been orderly and stress free. So, he decided that all he had to do was to eliminate these two women from his mind. And he resolved to embrace solitude. He would forbid himself to fall in love; he would only spy on the world of romance, writing about disappointments and sadness in the lives of others: good men who needed good women and vice versa. He would explore the stories of beautiful girls who took love for granted while the ugly and the mature desperately sought it. He would write about all the unwanted people of the world who refused to find happiness in solitude, but continued to enslave themselves to a futile quest for romance in a world that could never be sympathetic to them.

He wrote all these commitments down, and when he finally stood up, he felt a wave of relief nourishing his heart. If love came his way he would embrace it, but seek it, no. It would be hard, but he was ready.

He went outside, stood under the peach tree, and stared at the beautiful bond houses on the other side of the street. A young couple passed down the street before him. And then the gate of the durawall which enclosed the bond houses creaked open and he watched as two women came out and walked away. Shortly afterwards, two groups of girls arrived from opposite directions. They met in the street in front of him, stopped and chatted. All were beautiful, and he wished for them all, then he realised how delicious it was to feast with his eyes. This way, he thought, you can have as many girls as you want without any drama. He stood under the tree for a long time, triumphant at the prospect of an easy life behind closed doors, and without the expectation of happiness or glory, and with the inevitability of a solitary old age and death.

# Leftovers

My name is Thembalakhe Ncube. Some people call me Themba, for short. I hate it because Themba is a male name. But if you add 'lakhe' which means 'hers' in English, it becomes a female name. My friends simply call me Lakhe. I'm 27 years and seven months old. I live in the village of Gukwe with my parents, six siblings, my nine-year-old child and my grandmother. The village of Gukwe is one of the oldest villages near the city of Bulawayo. Nobody is employed in Gukwe except hawkers and fishermen; everyone wakes up to sit in the shade or loiter at the marketplace.

I had not been able to obtain tertiary education because my parents are poor. I was bright at school though, and I always did well in the end-of-term exams. I remember once my Form 1 teacher, G.K. Dube, saying regretfully that only if my father had enough money he'd do well to send me to university. My father hawked firewood in the townships of Bulawayo although business was bad because back then there was electricity. My father has never been employed in his life.

I have a child but no husband. I belong to a group of women called 'amazalakanye', which translates as 'leftovers' in English. Any woman with a child, who still lives with their parents after the age of 24, is called that. There are so many of us in Gukwe, you'd think it was fashionable. My friends Nomalanga and Thandiwe are also leftovers like me; women desperately seeking marriage. We've rival groups here in Gukwe, and when a promising man comes along, we compete to have him in our group and then compete amongst ourselves. Once my two friends ended up fighting over a man who turned out to be just all palaver like most men are. He had first showed an interest in Thinasonke before seeing Nomalanga, who's had her face painted yellow with skin lightening creams. He wanted to switch but Thinasonke thought Nomalanga was stealing her man, and they fought, after which Thinasonke stopped being our friend.

It's hard to decide whether a man is serious or just a casanova. Some of them talk good things but change their language once they've slept with you. The best thing to do is to have as many as you can so you don't miss a good one while stuck with a player. Some say that's what makes men run. I don't believe it. I believe that if a man really loves you, he'll try to keep you at all costs. I used to have a friend called Nompilo and she was considered a whore because she loved any man who wooed her. Yet now she has a husband with whom she lives in Jo'burg; she dumped all her other boyfriends when she found him. She's an inspiration to all of us. My friend Nomalanga is one of the new village whores. She's in touch with seven men right now; she'd have had more if she were wooed more often. I have one man because I trust him and I decided to end things with the other two when I found him. It's only holier-than-thou Thandiwe who has a single man and believes it's fashionable to do so. I wonder how she'll feel when this one drops her the way her baby-daddy did.

I met this man on a bus to Zintabeni. He boarded near Mguza and sat next to me. At first I didn't take any notice of him; he was just a short, nondescript man in 1970s short pants, coffee spectacles and brown *tekkies*. He joined the conversation brewing in the bus about *izinjiva* – young men who work in Jo'burg – about how they impregnate young girls and then leave them. Everyone spoke harshly against such heartless men, but he switched the blame to the girls. His boldness astonished me. He said that once in his village there was a very handsome girl whom he'd loved very much and whom he wooed for two years meaning to marry her, but she stubbornly turned him down. Yet when an *izinjiva* came along with his feigned Zulu accent, not only did she accept him, but she opened her legs for him, and he left her while she was still pregnant.

'Who would you blame in that case?' he asked everyone. We all looked at him speechless. He'd brown Mr-Know-It-All eyes and a round, tired face which was neither handsome nor ugly. When someone changed the subject, he jumped in and gave many examples of people he knew to be in similar circumstances. He was always at odds with everyone, giving fresh sides to every conversation, taking unpopular sides in arguments.

I think that's what attracted me to him in the first place. And when, finally, he turned to me, I was already won over. In a sort of whisper, he told me his name was Bafana and asked for mine. When I'd told him, he asked me where I was going, and when I replied, he told me – unasked – how he dealt in cattle, and was going to meet an associate at Nganga to strike a deal.

I was wearing my red dress which falls just below the knees, so it only reveals my shins. Some people say more is less and that's my code. I had my short hair combed nicely and no make-up, which is the way I like myself. I knew I was the best I could be, I was ready. I know my type, village men. Make-up puts them off, they think you're a whore. But to some of them, even less is too much.

As though we were old buddies who hadn't seen each other in a long time, he told me he'd once worked in a butchery in Cape Town, and how, after he accidentally cut several fingers off, he was made redundant without compensation because he was living in South Africa illegally. After that he told me, he returned home to live with his wife, but they'd had problems, 'so we separated three years ago.' He'd been to Canada, he continued, taking out his passport and showing me the immigration stamp. An unnecessary detail, I thought.

I looked at the hand with the lost fingers. It was a pitiful sight. And at that moment, I realized that I wanted the man more than anything. He could be my chance out of 'leftover-hood'. And it was easy to blot Sfiso and Mesabeni out of my mind.

We shared cell phone numbers before his stop, but then in a sudden change of heart, he said he would accompany me to Zintabeni, so that he could help me carry my purchases. I was going to buy *mbumbulu* at the Zintabeni market place.

'A lady like you shouldn't be alone,' he told me and I felt blessed.

Today is Friday, a month since we met. He's been calling almost every day, and I've come to know many things about him. I know he has two daughters aged ten and six with his ex-wife. He has sent me the picture of his homestead – a three-roomed white house, a kitchen hut and a granary. I also know that he plans to buy a truck very soon as his cattle business is doing well. This is the part that gave me confidence to break up with Mesabeni and Sfiso. Nothing is going to mess up this opportunity.

When I broke up with Mesabeni, I told him, 'This is the end of our affair. I can't continue seeing you.'

'Why? he exclaimed, 'Did I do something wrong?'

I said, 'No, it's me. I simply don't want to see you anymore.'

I could see how stricken he was. He begged me and did such disconcerting things that I can't mention them here. 'A girl has got to do what a girl has to do for her future', I stonily reassured myself.

Sometimes I marvel at the power we women wield over men and I wonder how it is that we get to be abused.

Sfiso was easier to break up with, and I hate him for that. He didn't even feign distress. He has other girlfriends. He just said if that's what I wanted, that was fine. I won't ever give him another chance even if we're the last two people left in the world. I like to see a man grovel, as Mesabeni did, when I decide to break up with them.

Some men refuse to accept when a woman decides to reject them. Thinasonke wanted to break up with her boyfriend from Macado Mine, after finding a *malayisha* boyfriend – who also turned out to be worthless. And it became war when the boyfriend from Macado threatened to kill this *malayisha* and accused him of coming all the way from Jo'burg to steal his woman. As if she were a piece of food. Imagine the insolence and contempt behind the suggestion that a human being can be stolen?

Today is the day that Bafana and I are to meet again. I'm seated with my friends Nomalanga and Thandiwe at my stand, waiting for him, and we've been waiting all day. We gossiped, criticised each other and laughed at other hawkers until we ran out of things to gossip or laugh about. Now we're seated waiting and we're tense. It's now 3 p.m. When he called me yesterday, he said I should expect him at 11 a.m. I've tried calling him thrice but his cell phone goes to voicemail. Once it rang without answer.

'Maybe he's in some kind of trouble,' Thandiwe says trying to reassure me. I make a face in response. Thandiwe is the best friend anyone can dream of having.

'Or he's on another date,' Nomalanga says laughing.

'Geez, have you no shame?' Thandiwe says, jabbing Nomalanga with her middle finger. 'Our friend is distressed and all you can do is add to her stress.'

'What? I'm saying it like it is. You can sugar-coat it all you want, but Lakhe here needs a reality check. I mean, come on Thandi, why has this guy not called if he's going to be late?'

Maybe he has problems he'll explain when he gets here.'

'And why is his cell phone switched off?'

'I don't know.'

'See. There're many things we don't know. So we've got to consider all possibilities. I think Lakhe here needs to hear the truth. And the truth is that she made a very big mistake by breaking up with her two soldiers. No soldier deserves that unless someone's put a ring on it.'

'Geez, do you have to be so insensitive?'

'I'm telling it the way it is. I've got seven soldiers. And they all love me. But not until one of them has put a ring on it, will I dump any of them.' Nomalanga giggles.

'That's you and your immoral ways, Noma. You can't expect Lakhe to behave like you.'

'Well let me tell you something Ms Holier-Than-Thou. When Phillip finally dumps you, you'll learn the biggest lesson in the world. That most men aren't worth it.'

Sensing a great war coming, I interfere. 'Okay guys. Enough! For your information Noma, I don't regret dumping Sfiso and Mesabeni. In fact…'

'Well I think you should, friend.'

It's always like this with these friends of mine – bickering and criticising each other. They're complete opposites. That's why it's always amusing to be with them. I don't think they'd ever have been friends without me.

The market place, which we call Sporo, is an immense area clustered with stands. It looks more like a reservoir that was paved after it dried up. It's a former taxi rank, and used to fill with all kinds of minibuses going everywhere in the country.

Behind most stands sit the Leftovers. They're easy to detect; their love for make-up and lightening creams betray them. But some, like Thando and me, are hard to notice. We don't like marketing ourselves to men, so we wear long skirts, wear no make-up and use no bleaching creams.

I sell fruit and vegetables. My stand is shaded with a tarpaulin awning supported by a metal framework. I acquired the capital to start my own business from my former employment.

Nomalanga and Thandiwe still work for other people. Their stands are next to mine. Before Nomalanga worked for her current employer, she worked for a man called Gatsheni. She lost her job when this Gatsheni slept with her. He fired her afterwards, saying that the fact of their having slept together would inconvenience their employer-employee relationship, so it would be better if they parted ways. I remember when she told us this, how shameless I thought she was. If it were me, I'd have been so embarrassed, I'd never have shared it with a soul.

Later in the afternoon, Mesabeni shows up and loiters near us, not greeting us, like a dog that has been chased away by its owner, though it hopes that by lurking nearby, the owner might decide to take it back. I feel both irritation and pity for him. I'm reminded of how I felt when my baby-daddy dumped me. For a whole month, I felt as if the world was over. I almost killed myself when I heard he was in love with another girl.

When five o'clock strikes and there's still no sign of Bafana, my friends and I rise and loiter, leaving MaNdiweni watching our goods for us. She's a meek elderly friend of ours, and she's only selling tomatoes.

First we go to the saloon because Nomalanga wants to check the new hair extensions. After that we loiter in the stands, just checking on the new stock. As usual, Nomalanga lags behind with a stranger. I only realise this when I try to show her the blouse that she'd said she wanted, which is offered at a discounted price. The man is tall and thin, handsome and beautifully dressed, though in cheap clothes. You'd think she known him way back, the way she's talking to him, smiling and laughing. Thandiwe and I share a look. Thandiwe seems appalled. I'm amused. We watch as Nomalanga gives the stranger her cell phone numbers before skipping to catch up with us, all smiles.

'You're a dog, Noma!

'Eh... sorry!'

'Don't sorry, me. You heard me. You're a dog!'

'Are you jealous?'

'Jealous? Do you even know that guy?'

'Yes. I know that he's hot, that he wants me. And that I want him.'

'What if he's a serial womaniser?'

'And aren't I a serial maniser?'

'Gross!'

I think you're jealous, Thandi. When was the last time a man stopped you and asked you for your phone numbers?

'I've a boyfriend. I don't pay attention to other men.'

Well, let me tell you why it's nicer to be me and it's so sad to be you. I don't wait for any man. I make men wait for me. And you...'

'At least I don't get to be a mat used by all men.'

When an argument breaks out between these two, it'll only stop if I intervene. So I do now, motivated by the grandmother who's listening to this bickering with interest.

Towards six o'clock I'm distraught as we head back to our stands. I wonder what could be the reason behind Bafana's failure to honour our date. I find myself only imagining the worst scenarios.

'Looks like someone is being stalked,' Nomalanga says as we turn by the last stand towards our own stands and behold, standing near my stand, his back to us, Mesabeni. He's wearing denim jeans and a navy blue football T-shirt. And has his hands in his pockets. I don't know how to feel. He wasn't dressed this way earlier.

'I forgot to tell you Lakhe,' Thandiwe says politely. 'Mesabeni has been begging me to put in a good word for him. I think the guy is distraught.'

'Which is why you should give the soldier another chance and stop acting holier-than-thou,' adds Nomalanga.

When we arrive at our stands, we thank MaNdiweni and start packing. Mesabeni doesn't greet us; he stands pokerfaced, as if in a dream. That's the way he is, though. Strangely, I feel his presence curing me of the anguish I've been caused by Bafana's failure to show up. It allows a new preoccupation to absorb my mind. After packing, I've to carry my merchandise to the house where it's kept for the night. It's half a kilometre away. I hire a trawler when the business is good, but today it's been a bad day, so I've to carry everything by myself, one bundle at a time.

'I can help you with that,' says a baritone voice while a large black hand take holds of the *mbumbulu* sack.

'I can manage.'

Mesabeni insists and I finally give up. I carry a roundnuts' sack. Glancing behind me, I can see Nomalanga and Thandiwe standing together beside Nomalanga's stand and staring raptly at us.

Along the way Mesabeni tells me, unasked, that he's happy because ZESA has finally reinstated him, so he's working again. I say nothing.

'We can still be friends Thembalakhe,' he continues. 'This animosity doesn't sit well with me. Especially given that I don't know what my crime is.'

It happens in a curious way, for no sooner has he finished saying this than I feel my heart melt towards him. I feel like he's slit his chest open and wrenched out his heart for me to see everything I want to see. His words echo in my head like advice from a sage.

'I'm real sorry Mesabeni,' I say. I want to continue and say that I didn't know that he felt so strongly about us, but that'd be effusive, so I restrain myself. Less is more, I quickly remember.

It'll take time before trust is restored between us, I know that. But I know, too, that with patience, it will. And once it has, and we're back together, ours would be a love that would blossom. There'd be one count less in the ever-growing number of leftovers.

Printed in the United States
By Bookmasters